"You've turned this house into a home, P.J."

"It was a home when I got here."

He shook his head. "Nope. Not even close," he said. "How do you do it?"

Shyly she said, "I suppose it's just because I'm a woman."

She'd meant the remark in the most innocent way. But the feelings it generated in him went from touch-and-go to downright dangerous.

"It's easier for women," she said. "We're naturally nesters. We pull in a bit of this, a smidgen of that, and—" she threw her arm out in a circular motion "—voilà. A building becomes a home."

And when she left at the end of the summer, the nest would go back to being just bits of this and that with no one to breathe life and vitality and warmth into it. This home would be a ranch again. And he'd be a footloose cowboy once more.

Isn't that what he'd always wanted?

Dear Reader,

The wonder of a Silhouette Romance is that it can touch *every* woman's heart. Check out this month's offerings—and prepare to be swept away!

A woman wild about kids winds up tutoring a single dad in the art of parenthood in *Babies, Rattles and Cribs... Oh, My!* It's this month's BUNDLES OF JOY title from Leanna Wilson. When a Cinderella-esque waitress—complete with wicked stepfamily!—finds herself in danger, she hires a bodyguard whose idea of protection means making her his *Glass Slipper Bride,* another unforgettable tale from Arlene James. Pair one highly independent woman and one overly protective lawman and what do you have? The prelude to *The Marriage Beat,* Doreen Roberts's sparkling new Romance with a HE'S MY HERO cop.

WRANGLERS & LACE is a theme-based promotion highlighting classic Western stories. July's offering, Cathleen Galitz's *Wyoming Born & Bred,* features an ex-rodeo champion bent on reclaiming his family's homestead who instead discovers that home is with the stubborn new owner...and her three charming children! A long-lost twin, a runaway bride...and *A Gift for the Groom*—don't miss this conclusion to Sally Carleen's delightful duo ON THE WAY TO A WEDDING.... And a man-shy single mom takes a chance and follows *The Way to a Cowboy's Heart* in this emotional heart-tugger from rising star Teresa Southwick.

Enjoy this month's selections, and make sure to drop me a line about *why* you keep coming back to Romance. We want to fulfill *your* dreams!

Happy reading,

Mary-Theresa Hussey

Mary-Theresa Hussey
Senior Editor, Silhouette Romance
300 East 42nd Street, 6th Floor
New York, NY 10017

Please address questions and book requests to:
Silhouette Reader Service
U.S.: 3010 Walden Ave., P.O. Box 1325, Buffalo, NY 14269
Canadian: P.O. Box 609, Fort Erie, Ont. L2A 5X3

THE WAY TO A
COWBOY'S HEART

Teresa Southwick

Silhouette
R O M A N C E™
Published by Silhouette Books
America's Publisher of Contemporary Romance

For my brother Dan Boyle and his wife, Katie.
Your laughter, loyalty and love is always an inspiration.
Thanks for the verbal crash course, no pun intended, in
horseback riding. I'm grateful that you didn't call me
crazy for asking, "But he could touch her leg now, right?"

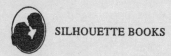

SILHOUETTE BOOKS

ISBN 0-373-19383-1

THE WAY TO A COWBOY'S HEART

Copyright © 1999 by Teresa Ann Southwick

Visit us at www.romance.net

Printed in U.S.A.

Books by Teresa Southwick

Silhouette Romance

Wedding Rings and Baby Things #1209
The Bachelor's Baby #1233
A Vow, a Ring, a Baby Swing #1349
The Way to a Cowboy's Heart #1383

TERESA SOUTHWICK

is a native Californian with ties to each coast, since she was conceived in the East and born in the West. Living with her husband of twenty-five years and two handsome sons, she is surrounded by heroes. Reading has been her passion since she was a girl. She couldn't be more delighted that her dream of writing full-time has come true. Her favorite things include: holding a baby, the fragrance of jasmine, walks on the beach, the patter of rain on the roof, and above all—happy endings.

Teresa also writes historical romance novels under the same name.

Dear Reader,

Relatives. Gotta love 'em. Right?

I was one of six kids in a close-knit family. My brothers and I still get together one weekend a year, without spouses and children, to reconnect. We actually *like* each other.

My husband and I tried to give our two sons the foundation of family that we both enjoyed. Then along came their teenage years. The kids tried to grow up while we struggled valiantly to keep them little *and* convince them that we knew best. I found that often what I didn't say was more profound than platitudes tuned out by selective teenage hearing. There were times when we fought, but we always loved each other. We were always family, and that relationship—good or bad—shapes our lives.

This is the theme of *The Way to a Cowboy's Heart*—a father's stern discipline and a rebellious teenager's interpretation that he's no good. Cade McKendrick is convinced that he has nothing to offer anyone, including the teenagers he's forced to take in for the summer. He hires single mom P. J. Kirkland as a cook and she soon sets out to show him he's one of the good guys.

Because family has always been such an important element in my life, I'm very proud that *The Way to a Cowboy's Heart* is included in FAMILY MATTERS, Silhouette Romance's promotion this month. I fell in love with Cade McKendrick and hope this cowboy finds his way into your heart too.

Teresa Southwick

Chapter One

"**Y**ou're a woman."

"You're a man." P. J. Kirkland shot back, then winced after the words popped out.

Open mouth, insert foot. The first time she'd laid eyes on her new boss too.

Would she ever learn to think before letting words come out? Cade McKendrick didn't seem a warm, fuzzy—forgiving—sort of man. She was relieved when his lips curved up slightly in a smile.

"Can't argue that." He glanced down at the paper on the desk in front of him. "I just figured P. J. Kirkland was a guy."

"That happens a lot."

"Hmm." The leather chair creaked loudly as he sat down. Not surprising. His approximately six-foot-two-inch, solid-as-a-rock frame would make any piece of furniture groan. Not to mention most females she knew. Luckily, she was the exception.

A good-looking man held no appeal for her. Not

anymore. But she couldn't help noticing that Cade McKendrick, with his deep blue eyes, sun-streaked brown hair and chiseled jaw, would not have to wear a bag over his head in public—unless he *wanted* to avoid female attention.

P.J. held out her hand. "It's nice to meet you Mr. McKendrick."

"Cade," he said leaning forward to squeeze her fingers. He indicated the chair in front of his desk and said, "Please sit down. What does P.J. stand for?"

"Would you believe pajamas?"

"No."

So much for trying to distract him with humor. Although brief, that flash of amusement on his rugged face moments ago had charmed her, and she'd hoped to bring it out again. But it was gone, as if it had never happened, replaced by an unreadable mask. He watched her intently, expectantly, waiting her out. He was going to make her tell him her full name. She would make him pay.

"Penelope Jane," she said quickly. "It's nice—"

"What's wrong with Penelope Jane?" Even as he innocently asked, the corners of his eyes crinkled slightly as his mouth twitched. She had hoped to impress him with her razor-sharp wit, not her dippy name.

She sighed. "Sounds like a character from a bad Doris Day movie."

"What's wrong with Penny?"

"Too cutesy. My older brother started using the initials and it stuck."

"Okay. So tell me what you know about kids."

"In twenty-five words or less?" she joked.

"Okay."

He sounded serious. P.J. frowned. Her experience and qualifications were in the résumé she'd sent him. Now that she thought about it, the fact that she was a woman was clear in her introductory letter. But maybe this was his way of breaking the ice.

"I teach high-school kids. Just completed my fourth year." Her job in Valencia, California, was a far cry from his ranch near Santa Barbara. Hard to believe the two places were in the same state, only a couple hours apart by car.

He nodded, apparently satisfied. "You can cook, right?"

Shouldn't this have been ironed out before she arrived? "If I couldn't, I wouldn't have answered your ad, in spite of the fact that this job is exactly what I need. The idea of a youth summer program on a ranch is innovative and a terrific opportunity. For children," she added, knowing she was babbling. She was nervous. She couldn't help it. He kept looking at her with those blue eyes that seemed to read every secret she had.

"These kids aren't children. They're teenagers," he said. "What's your specialty? In food, I mean."

"I don't do gourmet/fancy. But I know what kids like—hot dogs, hamburgers, tacos and fries are about as sophisticated as they get. I can make biscuits from scratch that will melt in your mouth. And my chocolate chip cookies wouldn't be mistaken for hockey pucks," she added, sacrificing modesty for honesty and complete objectivity.

Small doubts began to creep in on her. This felt an awful lot like a job interview, but she'd been under the impression that she already had the position. He'd left the message on her answering machine that she was hired and the date he wanted her to start.

She was about to ask a few incisive questions of her own when there was a loud crash outside his office door. P.J. jumped up and raced into the hall with Cade right behind her. There beside an antique accent table, she saw her daughter, Emily, with a shattered crystal photo frame on the distressed-oak floor at her feet.

"Mommy—" Her child's fearful gaze darted to Cade just before she scurried forward and buried her face against P.J.'s jean-clad leg.

P.J. crouched down and gathered the seven-year-old in her arms. "What happened, sweetie? I told you to sit quietly and not touch anything while you waited for me."

"Mommy?" Cade frowned. "You brought a kid with you?"

"Not a kid. My daughter, Emily." P.J. took a deep breath to keep her anger at bay. How long before she learned that when something looked too good to be true it usually was? Case in point: a job on a ranch where she and Emily could live for the summer. It had seemed ideal. She would be able to work and still save money on child care. She might actually get ahead financially.

She glared up at him. "I stated clearly in the letter accompanying my résumé that I had a child. I told you she would be coming with me. When you left the message that I had been hired, I assumed that you had gone over my qualifications carefully. But you haven't even looked at my résumé, have you, Mr. McKendrick?"

Before he could answer, Emily looked at him with

red-rimmed green eyes. Her lips quivered when she said, "I—I'm sorry about the picture, mister."

He went down on one knee and lifted the photograph from the shards of glass. He studied the granite features of the gray-haired man, then said, "Forget it."

Emily stared at the picture in his hands. "But it must be special—"

"Just my father," he said.

She rubbed a knuckle beneath her nose. "You're lucky. I don't have a daddy."

Her words tugged at P.J.'s heart.

"Me either. He died three months ago." He looked up at P.J. "Don't lose any sleep over it," he said reading the sympathy she knew was on her face. "I won't."

Emily sniffled again. "I'm extra sorry, mister."

P.J. pulled her little girl more protectively against her. "I'll see that the frame is replaced, Mr. McKendrick."

"Don't worry about it. And I already told you the name is Cade," he said, standing.

"I insist. As soon as—" She looked down when she felt a tug on her jeans pocket. "What is it, Emily?"

"Do ranches have bathrooms?"

Cade smiled for the second time in the last fifteen minutes. Once at her, once at Emily. He mumbled something that sounded a lot like "double trouble."

Great, she thought, already planning to apply for work at her local fast-food place. She would figure out some way to arrange child care.

When Emily tugged again, she said, "I'm sure there's a powder room. Let's ask Mr.—" she stopped when he slanted her a look. "Cade. He'll tell you where it is."

He pointed down the hall. "Go that way and it'll be on your right."

"Do you want me to go with you, Em?"

The girl shook her head, then looked uncertain. "But which side is right?"

"It's the side you hold your pencil. Okay?"

She smiled. "Okay."

They watched her until she'd found the right door, then P.J. turned to him. "You didn't answer my question. Did you read my résumé?"

He rubbed his neck. "No."

"Was mine the only one you received?"

He shook his head. "Got about six or seven."

"If you didn't read mine, how did you pick me?"

"Yours was on top."

"Would I be wrong to assume that you didn't check out my references either?"

"No."

"If I were a cowboy, would you have done some checking on my background?"

"Yes, but—"

She shook her head. This was no way to run a youth program. Cavalier and slipshod at best. "We're talking about children, not horses. This is irresponsible—"

"So I've been told," he said, bitterness twisting his words.

"I can't believe someone entrusted you with this program."

"Me either. But someone did."

"Who?"

"My father. It was his idea."

"And he passed away before he could get it running," she guessed. "I'm sorry for your loss, Cade. But this could be a dynamite thing you're doing. Channeling your energy into children will help you get over your grief—"

"That's what you think this is about?" he asked.

"Isn't it?"

"No." He ran a hand through his hair. "I hardly knew him. We hadn't spoken since I left home at eighteen. When he found out he was dying he sent for me. He ordered me to finish what he'd started."

"Ordered? You didn't want to?"

"Nope."

"Then why are you?"

"If I don't, I lose the ranch."

"I don't understand."

"If I don't see this program through the summer, the ranch will be sold and the money donated to his favorite charity." Cade watched her big brown eyes grow wider.

"You must have misunderstood—"

"His will was so clear I didn't even need the lawyer to translate." He shoved his fingertips into the pockets of his jeans. "He had already picked three kids from a local probation program. By the end of the summer, they'll go back where they came from and the ranch will be mine, free and clear. I just have to get through the next couple months."

Cade waited for her disapproving look. He wasn't disappointed. Her full lips tightened. Lifting his gaze slightly, he saw her nose wrinkle, drawing his attention to how freckle-splashed and turned-up-cute it was. A pale yellow cotton blouse tucked into her jeans showed off her slender curves. Shoulder-length brown hair curled in layers around her pretty face. She wasn't drop-dead gorgeous, but clean-cut and appealing. Not his normal type, although under different circumstances he might have been tempted to put moves on her. But she had a kid. That was strike one. Strike two: he had a bad feeling P. J. Kirkland was a do-gooder who would give him what-for about his attitude.

When she took a deep breath, he braced himself. Sometimes he hated it when he was right.

"Get through?" she said, clearly offended. "That's not good enough. These are children. They're at risk. You have a unique opportunity. This is a chance to make a difference in their lives. And you just want to 'get through'?"

"That's about the size of it." He didn't care whether or not she approved. He just needed her until the end of August. "So you still want the job, or do I need to call the second résumé in the stack?"

She blinked. "You're hiring me?"

The sound of footsteps kept her from saying more, and they both turned to see Emily coming toward them. The child stopped beside her and looked from P.J. to him. "Mister, if you have a broom, I'll sweep up the glass. Mom always makes me clean up my messes."

"I have a broom. You can sweep it into a pile, but don't pick it up. I'll do that so you don't cut yourself."

She glanced at her mother. "Is that okay, Mom?"

"It's fine," P.J. said.

"Good," he answered pointing. "The kitchen is that way. Follow me."

He started toward the back of the house when the

little girl slipped her small hand into his. It was amazingly small, and wet from a recent washing. Surprised, he looked down at her and she smiled. Glancing over his shoulder, he checked to make sure P.J. was following.

"I've never seen a cowboy before," she confided.

"I've never seen a little girl before."

She stared up at him, doubt written all over her small oval face. "You're fibbing, mister."

"Call me Cade. And I'm not exactly fibbing. I've never been this close to a little girl." The thought bothered him a little. He wondered what else he'd missed out on because of his wandering life-style.

"Really?"

"Cross my heart," he said.

"Did you hear that, Mom?"

"I did, sweetie. Cade hasn't been around boys either, he says."

"Is that why you need my mommy to help you?"

Helping him made it sound more intimate than it was. Bottom line: he was the boss; she was the cook. He glanced at the woman on the other side of the little girl. "Yes."

"At least you know when you're in over your head," P.J. said.

"Does that mean you'll stay for the summer?" He hoped the answer was yes. It would be convenient if he didn't have to find someone else on such short notice.

"I don't have a choice."

"How's that?"

She sighed. "I need the work."

Bright-eyed with excitement, Emily tipped her

head back and looked from him to her mother. "So we don't have to go?"

"No. As a matter of fact, I think we have a duty to stay." P.J. shot him a meaningful glance. "We have to help him get to know kids."

Emily frowned. "I don't know how. Travis Wilkins always pulls my hair. I ask him nicely to stop, but he won't. How can I help Mister Cade?"

"By doing what you're told," P.J. said.

The child nodded. "I can do that."

Cade shook his head, mystified. As easy as that she would behave, he thought. But his cynicism quickly returned. Emily was young yet. Give her time. Rebellion would set in and he'd like to be around to see Ms. Cool, Unruffled, Idealistic P. J. Kirkland deal with that. If Emily was half as much trouble as he'd been, he figured her pretty mother would have her hands full.

They entered the kitchen and he watched P.J. look around what would be her territory for the next three months. The approving light in her chocolate-brown eyes told him the spacious ceramic tile countertops and center island work area appealed to her. The side-by-side refrigerator would hold plenty of food for the three boys who would be boarding for the summer. The only thing he knew about young boys was how much they could eat—*that* he remembered. At the far end of the room, sitting on the oak-plank floor, was a table with eight chairs. That should give them enough space for eating.

He reached into the closet beside the pantry and pulled out the broom, handing it to Emily. "This is pretty big. Can you carry it?"

"Yes, sir." She tilted her head back to look at him,

then quickly glanced away. "Mister Cade, can I ask you something?"

"I guess."

"Will I fall over backwards if I look up at you all the way?"

"Why do you ask?"

"You're awful tall. I feel like I'm gonna tip over backwards if I do."

"I promise if I see you going over, I'll grab you. Fair enough?"

She nodded. "Can I ask you something else?"

"Sure. Shoot."

"Do you have a boy or girl of your own?"

"No." Cade stared at her, not sure where that had come from.

P.J. quickly ran interference. "Emily, you're procrastinating. It's time for you to go start sweeping up."

Cade raised an eyebrow. "Do you understand those twenty-dollar words?" he asked the little girl.

"Not always. But Mom helps me." She smiled at him. "You're really a cowboy?" she asked doubtfully.

"Yes." Hadn't they already covered this?

"But you're not wearin' a hat."

"You don't have to wear a hat to be a cowboy."

"But on the way here in the car, Mommy said cowboys wear hats. Do you?"

"Yes."

"White or black?"

P.J. moved forward and put her hand on the girl's shoulder. "Enough questions, chatterbox. Go clean up your mess."

"I will, Mom. First I gotta know what color his hat is."

"Brown," Cade answered.

Emily's forehead wrinkled as she thought that over. "Does that mean you're a good guy or a bad one?"

He mulled that for a moment, then answered truthfully. "Bad."

After reading Emily a bedtime story, P.J. wandered out on the front porch. Cade had put them upstairs in the room next to his. There were two other bedrooms down the hall from her and Em where the boys would stay. With a sigh, she sat on the swing. Suspended by thick ropes, the redwood frame was covered with a cushioned canvas pad. Moonlight combined with the lamplight spilling through the window to bathe her surroundings in a silver glow. Sighing again, she closed her eyes and relaxed her body into the cushy softness as she swayed gently back and forth. It had been an unsettling day, but this peace and serenity almost made up for it.

"Evening."

Her eyes snapped open. The sound of that familiar deep voice shot tension up her spine faster than she could say this town ain't big enough for the both of us. He was just emerging from the shadows beyond the circle of light from the house. "Cade. I didn't know you were out here."

"Didn't mean to startle you." He walked up the steps. "Before sundown I always do a last look-see around the ranch to make sure everything's quiet."

"Emily asked me to tell you good-night."

"She settle in all right?" he asked, removing his brown hat.

She remembered his words about being a bad guy. She didn't buy it. Would a bad guy care if a little girl was all right, or pick up her mess so she wouldn't cut herself? He leaned back against the porch support beam, and rested one hip on the railing beside her. It was a blatantly masculine pose that did strange things to her stomach.

"She couldn't keep her eyes open long enough to hear the end of her favorite story."

He set his hat on his thigh and rubbed the brim between his fingers. P.J. would never peg him as the nervous type, but, all the same, she sensed that something was eating him.

He cleared his throat. "If I gave you a bad moment today, I apologize, P.J."

"What do you mean?"

"About the job and all. With the kid to think about, and needing the work since your husband passed away—"

"What?" she asked, sitting forward on the swing.

"Emily said she didn't have a dad. I just assumed he was— You know."

"He's alive and well. I need this job because it allows me to save money on child care. Even if I could find it now. All the good camp programs are full by the time summer starts."

"What about her dad?"

"I support Emily by myself."

"He doesn't see her or help out?"

The mingled surprise and outrage in his voice startled P.J. Earlier she had thought him slipshod and actually called him irresponsible. Geez, she didn't know what to make of this man who was obviously steamed about Emily's absentee father.

Thoughts of Dave Kirkland steamed her up too. Annoyance vibrated through P.J., pushing her to her feet. "I don't want him seeing my daughter."

"Did he hurt her?" His voice was just this side of an angry growl.

"Not physically." She folded her arms over her chest, wondering why she was going to tell him. There was no reason she should, but the words still came pouring out. "He's a charming, good-looking airhead. Flaky as a French pastry."

"What did he do?"

"It's more what he *didn't* do. He was forever making plans to see Em and not showing up. I couldn't stand to see the disappointment on her little face when he broke promise after promise." She wrapped a strand of hair around her finger and was irritated to see that her hand was trembling. "To his credit, he was the one who decided to bow out and stop hurting her. At least he knew his limitations."

"How did Emily take it?"

"It's been a couple years since she's seen him. She appears to have accepted the situation." Better than I did in her shoes, P.J. thought. But thinking of her daughter made her smile. "Sometimes she seems far too mature for her age."

"That so?" he said.

She glanced at him. "She's had to grow up fast, maybe too fast. Sometimes I wish she could be a completely carefree kid."

"You? Miss Take-Your-Responsibilities-Seriously."

She grinned sheepishly. "I'm sorry if I came on a little preachy. I just like kids. I believe every one deserves a chance."

"So do I. With someone else."

Puzzled, she shook her head. "You're so cynical. Beats the heck out of me why Emily's taken such a shine to you."

"Me?" he asked, sounding shocked. "She has?"

"Just ask her."

"No, thanks."

His rigid posture drew P.J.'s gaze to the impressive width of his shoulders and chest in his plaid work shirt. Moonlight accentuated his rugged face and the frown he wore so comfortably. The pain she saw in his eyes tore at her. He was clearly a man in conflict.

He looked at her. "That little girl's had enough heartbreak. She shouldn't go asking for trouble from this cowboy." He shook his head. "It's like you said earlier, at least I know when I'm in over my head."

P.J. appreciated his honesty and sensitivity. On the other hand, she wondered why he would head for the hills, emotionally speaking, because a little girl had a small case of hero worship.

She shook her head. The last thing she wanted was to get involved with any man. Especially a handsome, complicated, mysterious cowboy. On the one-to-ten danger scale, Cade McKendrick came in a whopping fifteen. His problems were his business. Her problem was this job.

"So the boys arrive tomorrow?"

"That's right," he said.

She sat down on the swing again and moved slowly back and forth. "This is a wonderful thing your father started."

He heaved himself away from the porch railing and set his hat back on his head. Turning away, he tucked his fingertips beneath his arms and stared out toward the ranch buildings. "If you say so."

"You don't think it is?"

"It's not that. I'm just the wrong man for the job."

"Apparently he didn't agree."

He laughed, but it was a bitter, chilling sound. "He was determined that those boys not be disappointed."

"You sound surprised at that."

"I am." He turned and walked over to the swing, sitting down beside her. "Even more than his manipulation."

"Manipulation?"

"He knew how much I love this ranch. He was counting on that to get his way."

"Why did he feel emotional blackmail was necessary? This project was obviously important to him. Why couldn't he simply ask his only son to fulfill his dying request?"

She shifted her position on the swing and her thigh brushed against his. Ignoring the flash of heat and sparks, she forced herself to concentrate on the man beside her.

"He couldn't forgive me for being less than perfect."

"I'm sure he loved you, Cade." A man altruistic enough to give delinquent teens another chance would surely care about his own son.

Cade's mouth turned up in a bitter smile. "How could you understand? I bet your idea of doing something wrong is whispering in church, or not making your bed every day."

"You certainly have a strong opinion of me based on several hours acquaintance." She frowned at him. "Do you really believe I'm that one-dimensional?"

"Yeah."

"I'll have you know I got into my share of trouble."

Genuine amusement glinted in his eyes and relaxed the tension in his body. "Oh yeah? Define trouble."

She thought hard. "All right. I've got one. There was the time I was necking in the driveway with Bill Perkins. My brother came out, tapped on the car window, and told me to get in the house."

He laughed. "I bet that put a crimp in your social life for a spell."

"I was grounded for a month. Can you top that?"

"Lady, you don't want to know."

"Try me. I'm not the Miss Goody Two-Shoes you apparently think I am."

All traces of laughter disappeared. The black look was back and with it the tension. "All right. You asked for it."

"Well, what did you do?"

"Grand theft auto."

Chapter Two

"**Y**ou stole a car?" she asked in amazement.

He took little satisfaction from shocking her, even though he'd set out to do exactly that. "My father's car. Truck to be exact."

"What happened?"

"He made sure I was punished to the full extent of the law."

"But it was your father's. It was hardly more than borrowing the family wheels."

"I didn't have my old man's permission." He shook his head. "If it'd been the old days, he would've led a necktie party."

"You're exaggerating."

"You didn't know Matt McKendrick."

"No, I didn't." She stared out into the night for a few moments, then looked at him. "So I can only call 'em as I see 'em. *You* turned out all right."

That surprised him. "How do you know that?"

"I'm a pretty good judge of character." Her generous mouth turned up at the corners. "Except for one notable exception."

"Your husband."

"Ex-husband," she corrected.

So she was divorced. She hadn't mentioned that before. He had no right to be pleased by the information. He didn't want to be glad that the man was out of her life.

But damn it he was—pleased *and* glad.

The realization scared the hell out of him. He stood abruptly. "Time to turn in. Sunup rolls around fast."

"You have to be up that early?"

He nodded. "On a ranch, we need to use all the daylight there is."

She stood up, too. Taking a step toward him, she was close enough that he could smell the sweet scent of her hair and the fragrance of her skin. Need slammed into him, an ache to touch her and see for himself if she was as womanly soft as she looked.

The instant he'd laid eyes on her, he'd wanted to kiss her. For the second time in less than twenty-four hours his new cook gave him ideas, things no boss should think about an employee. Only now he was finding it even harder to resist the impulse. He was right to be afraid of her.

"I'll have breakfast ready for you," she said.

"No." The word came out more sharply than he'd intended.

A puzzled frown wrinkled her forehead, but she said, "I don't mind."

The last thing he needed was to see her, first thing in the morning. She tripped warning signals in his head that even a cavalier cowboy like himself couldn't miss.

"Sleep in, P.J. You're going to have your hands full when the boys get here tomorrow."

Several days later, while staring down hostile glares from those three disgruntled teenagers, P.J. understood the full impact of Cade's words. Since the boys' arrival, he had been too "busy" on the ranch to spend any time with them. The task of supervision had fallen to her. Fresh out of ideas for keeping them occupied, she had decided they could help with her chores.

She found out quickly that housework wasn't high on their top-ten list of exciting ranch activities.

"Learning to cook is a good skill to have. Someday you'll be on your own."

"When do we get to see this place? I didn't bust my ass staying out of trouble so I could come here and bake cookies." Steve Hicks, blond, blue-eyed and nearly six feet tall at seventeen, was the leader of the group. He sported a small gold hoop in his left ear.

"Me, either." Todd Berry, shorter than his buddy, with light brown eyes, agreed.

The third member of the trio, Mark Robinson, nodded. He was less vocal than the other two. Almost as tall as Steve, he always wore a baseball hat.

"I don't know what to say, guys." She held a bowl filled with cookie dough as she spooned it onto sheets for baking.

Standing on a chair beside her, Emily reached into the dough and plucked out a chocolate chip. After popping it into her mouth, she said, "I bet Mister Cade would know what to say."

P.J. wasn't so sure about that. But one thing she knew. He was trying to pass the buck, smack into her back pocket. She didn't plan to let him get away with it. She didn't mind helping out, but she'd bet her last dollar that housework hadn't been his father's vision for this program.

"Baking cookies, for God's sake," one of them muttered. "We'll never live this down."

She looked at the three boys. "You've got a point."

"We do?" Mark glanced at Steve who lounged against the kitchen counter.

"Yeah, and if you'll take the cookies out of the oven when the timer goes off, I'll do something about this."

The three looked at each other and answered, "Cool."

"Mommy, can I stay here with Steve? Please?"

P.J. had observed the boy for the last couple days. He was hostile and standoffish with adults, but with Emily, he was gentle and kind. He had an enormous amount of patience with the little girl and her chattering. She would be fine.

"Do you mind, Steve?" When he shook his head, she smiled. "I won't be long."

With the assistance of one of the ranch hands, she found Cade in the barn. His long sleeves were rolled to just below his elbows and he was dirty.

"Something wrong?" he asked when he saw her.

"What was your first clue?"

"You look mad," he said simply.

"Good. Because I am." Through her anger, a smidgen of respect for him registered. In all the time she'd known Dave, he'd never once taken the time to figure out what she was feeling. One glance and Cade had pegged her. "I just want you to know you're not going to get away with it."

"What?"

"Don't play dumb now. I'm on to you. I signed on as cook, not camp counselor. You're not going to dump those boys in my lap."

"You're a teacher."

"So what?" she asked, mentally cataloging her work experience. Then the light went on. She gave him a disgusted look. "You still haven't read my résumé, have you?"

"No." He shrugged. "Why?"

"I teach English at St. Bridget's School for Girls."

"What difference does that make? Kids are kids. Just do teacher stuff."

"Here's a news flash for you, cowboy. These are boys and there's rebellion in the ranks. It was today's baking that put them over the edge. Eating is the only part of chocolate chip cookies they want. If I suggest a crash course on Shakespeare, I guarantee murder and mayhem will be the result."

"You're overreacting."

"They bent over backwards staying out of trouble to earn the privilege of being in your program. This is a ranch, for God's sake. Do you think it's fair to leave them cooped up in the house with an English teacher who moonlights as a cook?"

"I don't know what to do with them."

"Me either. Boys are beyond my sphere of expertise." She glared at him. "At least you were one once."

He scowled right back. "And I was bad at it. What do you want me to do now?"

"Draw them into your world."

"Ranching?"

"That's why they're here. Chances are they've never been within spitting distance of a horse. I haven't. I bet they can't ride. They probably don't know how to take care of animals, at least none that big. This is a new world to them."

"I don't know how to let them in."

"Let them do chores." She indicated his dusty jeans and shirt. "From the looks of you, you could use a little help."

"It's dangerous to have greenhorns underfoot."

"Just let them watch. They'll ask questions. It will evolve from there. At least try. You owe them that much."

You owe your father, she wanted to say, but decided that wasn't the best way to get through to him. His hostility toward the man was obvious. With her hands on her hips, she said, "Bottom line, Mc-Kendrick, this summer program is yours whether you like it or not. You're going to have to get involved."

"Do you treat your boss at St. Bridget's like this?"

She couldn't stop the smile that tugged at the corners of her mouth. "When Sister Mary Constance gets out of line, you bet I do."

She'd hoped to coax a smile out of him, but he only nodded, a troubled look on his face. "Send them out."

"Done." She started to walk away.

"Did you say there are fresh-baked cookies?"

"I did. Are you hungry?"

"Starved."

She swore he was staring at her mouth when he said that, and the gleam in his blue eyes had nothing to do with chocolate chip cookies. Then she decided her brain had malfunctioned in the heat. Or she'd spent too long cooped up in an all-girls school.

"I'll bring some food out. Unless you want to come up to the house?"

It was becoming her habit to take a snack out to him in the afternoon. He wouldn't take the time to come inside, more likely he was avoiding her. She enjoyed the break in household responsibilities. And, if she were honest with herself, she looked forward to seeing him during the day.

"I'll grab something at the house after I've worked with the boys a bit."

That was a surprise. "Something will be waiting for you."

"What are you grinning at?"

She shrugged. "Just wondering if you're beginning to realize that all work and no play makes Cade a dull— Well, you get my drift."

She had been about to say "boy," and thank God the word hadn't popped out. There was nothing boyish about him. He was all-man, the first to interest her in a very long time. A wounded man. The worst kind because she sensed that he could hurt back. Yet he touched a part of her that wanted to reach out to him.

If only she'd had a face-to-face interview with him. She never would have taken this job. Now she was stuck. All she could do was protect herself, and the best way to do that was stay out of his way as much as possible. Because she had a bad feeling that it would be easier than falling off a horse for Cade McKendrick to break her heart.

In practically one gulp, Cade downed the lemonade that P.J. had handed him late that afternoon. It was the sweetest tasting he'd ever had. Maybe it only seemed that way because the kitchen was cool and permeated with the lingering scent of baked cookies and freshly broiled burgers and hot dogs. Or maybe it was because she'd given it to him.

She had no idea how he watched and waited for her to bring him lemonade and cookies every day. He was starting to look forward to the distraction she provided. Partly because she was a good cook, but mostly because he liked her. Either way it was a dangerous combination. Still, she would only be there for a little while, just till the kids went back to school. What could happen?

"Would you like some more?" she asked.

When he nodded, she opened the refrigerator and pulled out the pitcher. Cade held out his glass and she put her hand over his to keep it steady while she poured. Strange, he thought. The glass was cold and moist, her fingers cool. Why the hell was he hot all over from that slight touch?

He leaned back against the counter as he drank more slowly and observed P. J. Kirkland. In his early years of ranch jobs and rodeo riding, he'd met a lot of women. He'd sized them up quickly and slotted each one into a category, like horses in stalls. Some were career women who turned up their noses at him since he wasn't upwardly mobile enough. Others were buckle bunnies who followed the circuit looking for a cowboy to warm their bed. The nurturing kind were the most touch and go. They were the ones who wanted a husband and kids.

He couldn't figure out where P.J. fit. She had a career nine months of the year. She already had a kid, and from what she said, there had been one man too many in her life. He'd bet a dollar to a doughnut that he couldn't pin the buckle bunny tag on her either. Earlier in the barn, he'd felt an almost overwhelming desire to kiss her. He'd wondered if she'd read the need on his face, as fast as she'd made her excuses and headed back to the house. Nope, she was no buckle bunny on the make.

He almost wished she was. She'd be easier to handle.

"How'd it go with the boys today?" she asked.

Before he could answer, the kitchen door opened, and the young people in question trooped into the room with Emily in hot pursuit. P.J. poured lemonade all around, waiting and refilling glasses as needed. When their most immediate need was taken care of, she sniffed and wrinkled her nose in distaste.

"Showers. Pronto."

"Do we have to?" Mark asked. There were lines of fatigue around his eyes.

"We don't smell that bad," Todd said.

"I'm going to skip the part where we argue that point," P.J. said. "Let's go straight to where I tell you no shower, no dinner. *¿Comprende?*"

"Yeah," they grumbled, setting their glasses in the sink just before leaving the room.

Steve lingered, and when he turned, there was suspicion and hostility in his expression. Cade had dished out that look enough times to know it when he saw it. But he'd never been on the receiving end before and it was damned uncomfortable.

"Do we get to ride the horses tomorrow, dude?" Steve asked.

Cade pointed at the kid. "Let's get something

straight. *You're* the dude. I'm the boss. We'll ride when I say so."

"What do you say about tomorrow?" P.J. asked.

Cade thought about the million things he had to do. He couldn't turn these city kids loose, and he didn't have time to nursemaid them. But he hesitated as he looked into the boy's cool blue eyes. Something about Steve Hicks disturbed him. Although anger wiped every other emotion from his face, Cade sensed the eager anticipation just below the surface. For some reason, he recognized that the boy was excited at the prospect of horseback riding. And he also knew if anyone pointed that out to him, he would deny it.

Cade looked at P.J. who also waited expectantly for his answer.

He shook his head. "You don't just get up on a horse and ride."

"No?" Steve folded his arms over his chest. He was beginning to fill out. He would be a strong man someday.

"No."

"Why not?"

"It takes time. There are things you need to learn first."

"Like what?" Steve asked, his expression dark, his tone cutting.

"You have to earn his trust. Then maybe you can find out how to saddle the animal. How to get him to move, to stop, turn right and left. How to—"

"So show us."

"I don't have time tomorrow."

"Then just let us do it."

"You can't." Cade shoved his hand through his hair.

"Why not?"

"Too dangerous." He stared the kid down even though if looks could kill, he would be six feet under. "You could get thrown, stepped on. Horses can get mean. I need to personally oversee everything and make sure you're ready."

"So do it."

"I already told you I don't have time."

P.J. glanced over her shoulder at him as she poured oil into a big pot. "Could one of your employees supervise?"

Steve's eyes briefly lit up. "Yeah. Why couldn't one of them teach us?"

"They have work to do." He sucked air into his lungs. "So do you. I've assigned chores to all of you. Remember?"

"Yeah."

"You never get something for nothing in life. You have to work hard to get ahead." The words sounded hauntingly familiar, but he didn't stop to think about that.

"Figures," Steve said contemptuously.

"What's that mean?" Cade asked.

"That I should have known better." He glared. "You don't want us here. You never did."

"Hold on—"

"Why should I? What'll you do? Send me back for telling the truth? What do I care?"

"This is strictly a safety issue," Cade said. Again, he got the feeling he'd had this conversation before.

"If you're worried about being sued if I get hurt, don't. Nobody cares that much."

Cade moved forward. "I do."

"Like hell you do." Steve stomped from the room.

Cade was about to stop him with a stern reprimand about a lady present, but the words never came out. Shaking off the weird, déjà vu kind of feeling, he glanced at P.J.

"You're mad again." He'd never been able to read a woman so fast and easily. But he'd never encountered such expressive big, brown eyes either.

"I am not," she disagreed. She rested her back against the countertop, ignoring the pot of oil she had heating on the stove.

"You're not upset about what just happened?"

"No."

Arms folded over her chest, and the rigid line of her mouth convinced him otherwise. It surprised him how much he wanted to put the teasing smile back on her face.

"Does Sister Mary Constance know you're a fibber?"

"She knows I do my job to the best of my ability and that I care about all the students in my charge."

"Why do I get the feeling we're suddenly talking about me?"

"Because we are. Do you like the kids?"

"I don't know them."

"You're not doing anything to change that either."

"What I told him was the truth."

"I believe you."

"Then what's the problem, P.J.? Why are you mad?"

"I'm not mad. Not exactly." She sighed. "He's crying out for just a little of your time."

"And I don't have any to give. Why can't you understand that? This is a working ranch, not a boys' camp. If I don't work, all of us go under."

Odd, he thought, that she'd figured out that Steve was begging for his time. He had understood that right away and wondered how she had known. But it didn't matter what he understood or why, he wouldn't get involved. Not with the kids or anyone else. He had nothing to give.

He looked into P.J.'s dark, troubled eyes. He wanted to erase the concern he saw in her face. Funny, he'd never cared before what anyone thought about him. But it was different with her. She'd only been there a short time and her good opinion mattered to him. That was a real bad sign.

Then again, why should he lose any sleep over it? He was running on empty and he had been for a long time.

P.J.'s anger evaporated as she watched the play of emotions over his rugged face. There were lines of fatigue around his mouth and circles beneath his eyes. She understood that running his ranch was a big job. She realized that squeezing in time for the kids was hard, and he had freely admitted the summer program was something he didn't want to do.

She wasn't mad at him as much as she was disappointed and confused. She watched Cade watch her until she couldn't stand it any longer. She walked to the refrigerator and pulled out a bowl of cut-up potatoes immersed in water to keep them from turning brown.

She needed something to occupy her hands, hold her nerves in check. The man unsettled her in so many ways she'd stopped counting. Why was he so reluctant to get involved with the boys? On top of that, he seemed to know what she was thinking almost before she did. He read her as easily as a digital thermometer. She sure wasn't used to anyone paying that much attention.

He moved behind her, close enough for her to absorb the heat of his body and smell the combined scents of hay, horses and cologne that she was beginning to associate with him. Her heart fluttered, and her knees felt about as solid as her cookie dough.

This was the worst, the most disturbing thing of all. The way she responded to his blatant masculinity was nothing short of humiliating. She'd sworn after Dave, she would never fall for a good-looking, emotionally unavailable man. She'd meant it too. But Cade McKendrick was different, and she wasn't even sure how. A minute ago, she had been mad at him for brushing Steve off. Now, she held her breath, alternately wanting him to touch her and praying that he wouldn't.

"I know you have work to do," she said. As she talked, she pulled potatoes from the bowl and dried them so the oil wouldn't splatter when she cooked. "But your father must have known what it takes to run a ranch. He set the program in motion and apparently felt that he would have time for all of it."

"Yeah. Strange, too, considering he never had time for me."

She turned around and looked at him. The expression on his face reminded her of Steve. He quickly shuttered his feelings, but not before she made a guess. "You're ticked off because your father had time for strangers, and not for you, his own son."

His eyes narrowed. "You teach psychology too?"

"No. But it doesn't take Freud to figure out what's going on."

"Maybe it does, because frankly, lady, you're not even in the corral on this one."

"No?"

"No." Blue eyes narrowed on her as he glared.

She was about to call him on that when her peripheral vision registered a bright flash. Her heart leaped as she realized that the pot of oil had ignited. "Uh-oh. Fire."

He whirled around. "Damn it! Where's the fire extinguisher?" Frantically, he started opening cupboards, looking for it.

Calmly, P.J. picked up the lid for the pot and carefully dropped it over the flames. Determining it was safe, she took potholders and lifted the kettle to a cool burner. When the smoke dissipated, she cautiously lifted the cover to make sure the fire was out. Satisfied that the cut-off-the-oxygen method of fire knockdown had been effective, she breathed a sigh of relief. Cade was still haphazardly searching above the refrigerator.

"What are you doing?" she asked.

He glanced at her. "Fire extinguisher. There's got to be one."

"It's called a lid."

"What?"

"The fire extinguisher. I just put the cover on the pot. The fire's out."

He glanced from her to the Dutch oven, and back again. As his body slowly relaxed from the near-crisis, he shook his head and grinned. "I don't believe it."

"What?"

"The way you did that."

"Not flashy, but effective." She wasn't sure if she was being insulted or not. "What did you expect?"

"A little more hysteria for starters. Then I wouldn't feel like such a jerk."

She smiled back. A compliment. "How often do you cook in here?"

He shrugged and said, "Almost never. I've only been back a few months."

"Then you'd have no reason to know the extinguisher is in the cupboard closest to the stove." She opened the door and pointed it out.

If she sidetracked him, maybe he wouldn't realize why she'd forgotten to watch the stove. He was far too good-looking for her peace of mind, and that dash of vulnerability she'd glimpsed had tugged at her heart, nearly pushing her over the edge. The crisis was her fault for not watching what she was doing. Thankfully it was nothing more serious that a ruined batch of oil.

With her unsettled feelings too close to the surface, P.J. couldn't look at him. She busied herself turning off the heating element on the stove. "Grease fires are the most common in the kitchen. The easiest way to smother them is with the pan lid."

"You sound like you know what you're talking about."

"I took a class."

"That's not on your résumé too, is it?" he asked, sounding annoyed with himself.

"No," she said, glancing up. She laughed at the look on his face. "You're off the hook on that. If you haven't read it by now, I don't hold out much hope that you ever will. Besides, if you're not happy with my work, at this point you'd just fire me."

"Haven't we had enough of that for one day?"

She chuckled, then stared at him. "You actually have a sense of humor."

"You sound surprised."

"I am," she agreed

And wary too. Western-movie-hero looks and a sense of humor to boot. A lethal combination. This was the first time she'd ever spelled trouble c-o-w-b-o-y.

Chapter Three

"Where's my mom?"

"Shopping for groceries." Cade looked down at the little girl beside him on the porch swing. She'd insisted on sitting there to wait for her mother. After the fire the previous night, P.J. had said there were things she needed from the store. Her exact words were, "The idea of three ravenous teenage boys is too ugly to contemplate."

"Why'd she go without me?"

He sighed. He'd already answered this one. "She was going to get you, but you were busy playing with the new kittens. I told her to go on, that I'd watch out for you."

"But she's been gone all day."

"Not quite." Although it felt that long. After thanking him repeatedly, P.J. had said she could shop much faster without Emily. Now he was beginning to wonder.

"What if the car broke?" Emily looked up at him, her green eyes begging for reassurance.

"It's fine."

"How do you know? What if she got a flat tire? Or the engine blew up?" She brushed a strand of hair, the same shade of brown as her mother's, back from her face. "Mommy doesn't know about that stuff. I heard her say so."

"If she was stuck, she'd have called."

"What if we were all outside?"

"There's a message machine. Did you check it?"

"Nope." She hopped off the swing. "I'll go look."

"Good idea." When the front door slammed behind her, Cade took a deep breath, bracing himself for the next go-around.

A moment later, she appeared at the screen door. "How do I know if there's a message?"

"Was the red light blinking?"

"No."

His stomach tightened. He'd hoped for word from P.J. "Then no one called."

"Where's Mommy?" She came outside and stood in front of him, her lower lip quivering.

He rested his elbows on his knees. "Buying groceries. Do you know how much boys eat?"

"I watched Steve last night. He had two hamburgers. Then he finished mine. Why didn't Mommy make French fries the way she usually does? Those weren't the best."

He thought about the fire and how competently she had handled the situation. She'd finally baked the potatoes. He'd thought they were pretty tasty. The ones she normally made must be a world-class ride.

"She couldn't do them the way she wanted to be-cause there was an accident."

"Accident?" Her eyes widened. "What if an ac-cident happened to Mommy? What if she's hurt? What if she couldn't call? What if she never comes back? What if—"

He tapped her nose. "What if you stop borrowing trouble?"

"What does that mean? Why would anyone borrow trouble? Does that mean you have to give it back?"

"When you're finished with it."

She grinned. "That's silly."

Her smile made him glad he'd been able to take her mind off things for a minute. But that didn't ease his own misgivings. P.J. had been gone a long time. But how long was too long when you were shopping for a week's worth of groceries for six people? He didn't have a clue. What if she *had* been in an acci-dent? What if she never came back? He didn't even know who to call to come get the kid. Did P.J. have folks? Where was Emily's father?

"It's not gonna work, Mister Cade."

"What's that?"

"Distracting me. Mommy says I'm not easily dis-tracted. Not like when I was little."

"Oh. You're big now?" He lifted her slightly, pre-tending that he could hardly heft her slight weight. She was no bigger than a minute. She giggled, then wrinkled her nose, showing him that she was on to him. He noticed the spattering of freckles across the bridge of her cute little button nose. Like mother, like daughter.

Where the hell was P.J.?

"I'm seven, almost eight. My birthday's before Mommy and I hafta go back home."

"Is that right?" He tugged playfully on one of her pigtails, just below where the pink ribbon fastened it. "What do you want for your birthday?"

"That doll with the big boobs." Then her eyes narrowed and she pointed one small finger accusingly at him. "You're doing it again."

"Distracting you?" It took every ounce of his self-control, but he managed to keep a straight face and not react to her description of the doll.

"Uh-huh." Her bottom lip pushed out. "I wish Mommy would get here."

"If she doesn't come back soon, I'll go look for her. Deal?"

"You promise?"

"Yup."

Just then, he heard the faint sound of a car. In case he was wrong about it, he didn't say anything so Emily wouldn't be disappointed. Finally, he saw a cloud of dust, then P.J.'s compact car roared up the circular drive and stopped in front of them. She hopped out, smiled brightly and waved, then unlocked the hatchback. She had a helluva nerve looking so cheerful after what she'd put her daughter through.

"I'm glad you guys are here," she said. "I could use some help with this stuff. I got some great—"

"Where have you been?" Cade walked down the steps and stood in front of her.

Emily followed and folded her arms over her chest. "We were worried, Mom."

"We?" P.J. looked at him and her right eyebrow rose questioningly.

"He was keeping me company," Emily said. "I

borrowed trouble and now I have to give it back because you're here. What took you so long, Mommy?'' she asked, throwing her arms around her mother's waist.

P.J. put her hand comfortingly on the girl's shoulder. ''I'm sorry you had a bad time. But it takes a while to buy enough food for growing boys.''

''That's what Mister Cade said,'' Emily told her, tipping her head back to look up.

''Did he?'' She glanced in his direction.

Cade could almost hear her asking questions. Like why he could find the time to reassure a little girl when the boys had practically begged him for a crumb of his attention. She wouldn't buy his explanation that this was different, but it *was*. Emily was a little kid and she was scared. End of story.

''Did you get enough for Steve to have two helpings?'' Emily asked.

''I got enough to feed a good-sized horse. See?'' she said, indicating the back of the car, chock-full of bags and assorted things.

Emily leaned in the opening and started rummaging through the packages. ''Can I help?''

''I expected you back a long time ago,'' Cade snapped.

P.J. stared at him for three straight seconds before turning away. She rearranged the bags and gave her daughter one that contained a loaf of bread, and a package of hot dog rolls. ''Here. This is really heavy. Do you think you can handle it?''

'''Course I can.'' She took her package and raced to the front door. ''Then I'm gonna go find Steve.''

''Is there a problem?'' P.J. asked Cade when the child had disappeared inside. ''Was Emily any trouble?'' She grabbed several bags and carried them up the front steps.

''Other than the fact that she could talk the ears off a bull elephant, no.''

''Did you need something?''

''No.'' He didn't want to go where that question could take him. He lifted groceries out and followed her into the house.

''So there wasn't a crisis here that only I could handle?''

They set their bundles on the kitchen counter and looked at each other. P.J. was a little breathless from carrying the bags.

''No,'' he answered.

''Then why are you acting like a wounded bear?''

''I'm not.''

''The heck you're not. And I don't understand why. You offered to let Emily stay here with you. So what's your problem?''

''What took you so long?'' He heard the irritation in his voice, and knew it sounded damn close to worry. It was too late to take back the words.

''I'll show you what took me.'' She brushed past him and he heard the front door slam. A few moments later it banged closed again. She entered the kitchen lugging a flat of fresh strawberries with a bouquet of mixed flowers on top.

''This is what took me so long.'' She dropped the crate on the table and glared at him. ''I stopped at a wonderful fresh-fruit stand by the side of the road. There's corn on the cob, oranges, and asparagus.''

''You couldn't get this stuff at the store?''

''Of course. But you can't buy fresh-picked quality in a supermarket.'' She lifted the flowers and inhaled.

The deep breath expanded her T-shirt and the curvy breasts beneath. His mouth went dry.

The involuntary, unwanted attraction to her hiked his temper up a notch. "Who cares about fresh as long as there's food, and plenty of it. Those three are like human vacuum cleaners. I don't think they taste anything anyhow. I expected you back a long time ago."

She gave him a sharp look, then her eyes widened in comprehension. "We're not talking about brussels sprouts and broccoli, are we? You were worried."

As soon as she said it, he knew she was right. Worse than that, he knew why. She got his attention because she was the first woman he'd ever met who didn't slot neatly into a single category. She was a career woman, mother and care-giver, all wrapped up in a buckle bunny's sexy body. She intrigued him. But he would unravel his favorite rope before he would admit any of the above.

He shrugged. "What was there to worry about? You're a big girl." Truer words were never spoken, he thought as his gaze drifted over her womanly curves. "You can take care of yourself."

"Who's fibbing now?" She grinned at him. "You don't need to say the words, it's enough that I know the truth. You're very sweet."

Impulsively, P.J. stood on tiptoe and kissed his cheek. Before he could stop himself, he folded her into his arms and pulled her close. The sensation of her breasts pressed against his chest sent heat coursing through him as he lowered his head and touched his lips to hers. His breathing quickened and when she opened her mouth he accepted the invitation and invaded with his tongue, exploring the sweetness she offered. He'd never experienced anything like this heart-pumping, raise-your-blood-pressure kind of kiss.

He was an idiot to do this. It was a fitting punishment for him to know beyond a shadow of a doubt that she was even softer than she looked, and tasted better than he'd dreamed. More than his next breath he wanted to deepen the kiss. That was exactly the reason he forced himself to pull away from her.

He ran his hand over his face. "I shouldn't have done that."

"It was my fault," she said.

Way to go, Kirkland, she thought disgustedly. It wouldn't have happened if she hadn't kissed his cheek. She had a talent for making an awkward situation ever so much more embarrassing.

He shook his head. "Let's not bat the blame back and forth. I just want you to know it won't happen again. And I'd appreciate it if you'd forget about this."

"Already forgotten," she lied. With trembling fingers, she touched her mouth, still swollen from his kiss. "Your secret is safe with me."

"What secret?"

"The one where you worried about me because I was late. Inside your chest beats a heart with a gooey marshmallow center." Trying to lighten the moment, she placed her hand over his chest and was surprised that there was nothing marshmallow-gooey about his heart. It was pounding like a jackhammer.

"A bald-faced lie." He swallowed hard, then quickly headed for the door. "I'll bring in the rest of the groceries."

"I'll give you a hand."

"No. Stay. You should start putting things away before the frozen stuff melts."

"Whatever you say, boss."

P.J. shook her head, puzzled. If someone had shouted, "Head for the hills, the bad guys are coming," she didn't think he could have moved away from her more quickly. On the one hand, it hurt her feelings. She had no illusions about being a raving beauty, but she didn't need to wear a brown bag over her head either.

On the other hand, his putting distance between them was for the best. She didn't trust herself to do it considering her fascination for Mr. Tall, Dark, Handsome, Man-of-Few-Words McKendrick. Her penchant to lead with her heart and think later had brought her Dave the Disaster. Growing up without a father should have taught her better, but she'd believed it would be different for her. Instead, she'd acquired the necessary lesson in the school of hard knocks. Now she had a child to think about. Em could get hurt again. P.J. knew she had no business permitting herself feelings for a man who clearly had issues in his past to deal with.

On yet another hand, his charm was just physical. Hold it right there, she told herself. That was three "hands." One had to go. The part where she was attracted. She would get it under control if it killed her, because the feeling was one-sided. She wasn't sure what had prompted that toe-curling kiss, but he'd sure left her in the dust quick enough. He'd probably already forgotten the feel of his mouth on hers, but she wasn't that lucky. It had been hot enough to brand the memory into her head and heart forever. If she wasn't careful.

* * *

"But, Mommy, why can't I go with Steve?"

"Because he's going to a movie with one of the ranch hands. Besides the fact that you weren't invited, it's too late for you."

"Todd and Mark get to go."

"They're older."

Emily plopped herself onto the leather couch in the living room and folded her arms over her chest. P.J. noted the thrust-out bottom lip and knew she was in for a serious pout. The little girl had taken quite a shine to the good-looking teenager. She prayed Em didn't take after her in affairs of the heart. Watching her child's feelings be hurt without going for the jugular of the guy who did it would take a more self-controlled mother than she.

"I'm old enough. I'm almost eight," she said.

"I know, Em. I was there from the beginning. That makes me the mom. And, in my opinion, you won't be old enough to go out after dinner for at least six, eight, twenty more years."

The glare she got was rife with animosity. It was times like these when P.J. wished she had a partner to take the heat off her. There was no united front for Emily to divide and conquer. It was just her, and Em could easily cut her off at the knees with a well-placed scowl.

"What's happening in twenty years?"

P.J. turned to see Cade in the doorway. "I didn't know you were there."

"Problem?" he asked.

"What was your first clue?" She heaved a big sigh.

He indicated the unhappy little girl on the couch with her back to him. "She's not asking questions."

"That's the upside to telling her no. She turns into a mute."

"Anything I can do to help?"

"Short of taking her to the movie, over my dead body I should warn you, I'm not sure."

He walked into the room. Passing the flagstone fireplace that took up most of one wall, he sat down on a wingback chair across from Emily. Between them was an oak coffee table. Cade leaned forward and rested his elbows on jean-clad knees. He wore a white shirt with the sleeves rolled up revealing wide, strong, tanned forearms.

With an effort, P.J. kept her breathing even and steady, and her heartbeat within normal limits. If he ever suspected her strong attraction, it would be too awkward to continue working for him.

"Movies aren't such a big deal," he said to the sulking child. "I bet we could find something to do around here that would be fun."

Emily glanced at him. "What?"

"There's a rumor going around that you were interested in one of the horses."

"Lady?" Her tone brightened considerably.

P.J. sat down in the chair beside Cade's. He had showered before dinner and the scent of his soap and aftershave drifted to her. She forced her attention to her defiant offspring.

"Was the rumor that I wanted to feed Lady? 'Cause that's what I want to do. Will you let me?" she asked.

He nodded. "I'll even show you how."

"Oh, boy!" Emily jumped off the couch, skipped around the coffee table, and launched herself into his arms.

Looking uncomfortable with the affection, Cade met P.J.'s gaze. "I take it that's a yes?"

"And then some. It's a miracle." She laughed at his blank expression. "Em is the Princess of Pout. She's come close to a Guinness Book record for long faces."

"Mom," the little girl said, propping one fist on her hip and leaving her other arm around Cade's neck. "You're exaggerating again."

"Maybe a little."

Emily grabbed one of Cade's large hands in her two small ones and pulled as hard as she could. "Let's go."

He stood up. "I guess we're going now."

Emily tugged him to the doorway then looked back at P.J. "Aren't you coming, Mommy?"

"I wasn't sure I was invited," she said.

"You have to come."

One corner of Cade's mouth lifted. "Sounds to me like a royal command from the Princess."

P.J. laughed. "Then it seems I have no choice but to tag along, before her sovereign regalness lops off my head."

Emily giggled. "You're silly, Mom."

The three of them walked outside. P.J. couldn't remember a more lovely summer evening. Crickets chirped as a pleasant breeze wafted the scent of hay, and jasmine, and roses around them. Emily ran ahead, leaving the two adults to stroll at a more sedate pace. The silence stretched on until it became awkward.

"It's nice—"

"She's really—"

As they both spoke at the same time, P.J. looked up at him and laughed. "You first."

"Nope," he said shaking his head. "Ladies first."

"You sound like a B-movie western hero. 'Shucks, ma'am, that ain't no way to treat a lady.'"

"There are two things wrong with that statement."

"What?"

"My old man would've knocked me from here to kingdom come for saying 'ain't.'"

"H-he hit you?" He'd indicated his relationship with his father was tense. Had there been physical abuse?

"Only with words." A muscle in his cheek contracted as he thought for a minute.

"What's the second thing?"

"I'm no hero." He looked down at her, and she could have sworn he dared her to contradict his words.

If he thought she wouldn't, he'd better think again. "Why do you insist on playing the bad guy?"

"I'm not *playing* anything."

"That's twice you've said what a big, bad hombre you are. What you *do* tells me something very different. You're a fake and a phony, Cade McKendrick."

"What are you talking about?" He stuck his fingers into the pockets of his jeans.

"A black-hearted outlaw wouldn't go out of his way to cheer up a disappointed little girl."

He shrugged. "Don't make something out of this. It's no big deal."

"I think it's very brave considering that you knew there was a better than even chance she would come out of her snit and ask a million questions."

She knew he'd responded to her bantering when he met her gaze, and the dark look of moments before was gone. He grinned. "Aw shucks, little lady, t'weren't nothin'."

"There you go, again with the sense of humor. Why do you hide your funny side?"

"I don't. Maybe no one brought it out before."

"Did you just say something nice to me?"

"Nope." He shook his head and gazed straight ahead, but she could see he was half-smiling.

"Have it your way."

Emily came running back. "What's taking you guys so long? Lady's waiting and she's getting awful anxious."

"Is she now?" Cade said.

Emily nodded emphatically. "She's hungry."

"And she knew you came to feed her?" P.J. glanced at Cade. "You could make a fortune with a telepathic horse."

He laughed. "Let's hurry then," he said to the impatient child.

His hesitation was only a half second when Emily slipped her hand into his. P.J. wasn't even sure why she noticed. But she gave him points for not pulling away from the little girl.

They entered the barn and Cade switched on an overhead light. He led Emily to a bin in the corner and opened it.

"Carrots are in here," he said. "Take two."

She did, then meekly followed him to the last stall on the right. Lady stood there, staring curiously at them over the gate.

Cade opened it and led them inside. The straw whispered beneath their feet as they walked to the horse. He bent over and took Emily's hand then flattened it out, making sure her fingers weren't curled into her palm.

"Keep it flat, Emily," he instructed. "Lady is the gentlest horse on the ranch. She wouldn't hurt a fly. But she could make a mistake if your fingers are sticking up. She might accidentally bite you."

"Yes, sir," Emily said solemnly.

The child followed his instructions, and very soon the horse took the hint. She nibbled the carrot from Em's hand and the child giggled.

"It tickles," Em said. "And her nose is soft."

"I'm glad you like her." Cade rubbed the horse's neck. This was the first time P.J. had seen open, unselfconscious affection from him.

"She's a beauty," P.J. said, moving to the other side of the animal.

"She ate the whole carrot in one bite," Emily crowed. "Can I give her the other one?"

"Sure. Just remember how I showed you." He patted the horse again. "Emily?" The child gave him her complete attention. "It's all right to feed Lady any time. But she's the only horse. The rest of them are high-strung and unpredictable. You need to stay away from them unless I'm with you. Okay?"

"I promise," she said seriously. "That carrot's gone too. Can I give her another?"

"Sure. I'll go get you one," he said.

When he left them, P.J. moved beside her daughter who tentatively stroked the horse's neck the way Cade had done.

"Mommy?"

"Emily?"

"This is serious, Mom."

"You have my undivided attention, kidlet."

"For my birthday? I changed my mind about the doll with the big—"

P.J. pointed at her. "Don't say it."

Emily grinned. "Okay. But you know the one I mean."

"I do. So what do you want instead? Anything has to be an improvement over that shallow standard of feminine beauty."

"I don't understand what that means, Mom. But this is definitely better."

"I bet you're going to tell me you want a horse, huh?"

The little girl shook her head. "No."

"Good. Because I hate to tell you this, but our house just isn't big enough for a horse. And the mess. What would the neighbors say?" She heard rustling in the hay behind them and knew Cade was back with the carrots. "So what is it? Your wish is my command, O Princess of Pout."

"I want a cowboy. For my daddy."

Chapter Four

Cade saw P.J.'s shoulders stiffen. She hadn't known what Emily was going to say. Firsthand experience had shown him the little girl said whatever was on her mind. He knew P.J. knew he had heard and she was as straightforward as her daughter. The chances were slim to none that they could just ignore this. Which was probably just as well. In case she had any crazy ideas about him and herself, now was the time to put a stop to it. But he couldn't help wondering what she would say, how she would handle the situation.

The last thing he'd expected her to do was hug the little girl. But she pulled the child into her arms and said, "Emily Elizabeth Kirkland, you are a piece of work."

In a muffled voice against her mother's shoulder, the kid said, "It's not very long till my birthday, Mom."

"I know, kidlet. But right now it's not very long

till bedtime." She set the child away from her. "Why don't you go brush your teeth and get ready? No argument."

"Okay." Emily kissed her mother's cheek, then walked over to Cade and looked up expectantly. She stood in front of him for several moments, waiting. Was he supposed to do something?

"Good night," he said.

"'Night," she answered and brushed by him.

Cade had the feeling he'd failed some kind of test, but wasn't sure what it was. The hay rustled as P.J. stood.

"You heard her birthday wish." It wasn't a question. But when he nodded, she still winced and the pink in her cheeks deepened slightly. "I hope you don't think it has anything to do with you," she said.

"Of course not. An English teacher from St. Bridget's must know at least half a dozen single cowboys," he commented wryly.

"I trip over them constantly. You can't turn around without bumping into one. It's so annoying."

"I can imagine."

She shook her head sheepishly. "Look, Cade. There's something you need to know. Em has a mission in life and she's become an expert."

"At what?"

"Embarrassing her mother. I'm completely mortified."

"Don't be."

"That's a tall order because she has another mission which she pursues with single-minded determination."

"Finding a dad?" he asked.

"What tipped you off? Not much of a stretch, I

suppose, after what you overheard. I hope you don't—"

"I don't."

"You didn't let me finish."

"Didn't have to." He stuck the tips of his fingers into his jeans pockets. "Emily's a great kid. I hope she gets what she wants."

"In most things I would agree."

"As long as you understand it's not me."

She frowned. "What are you—"

"She deserves the best and I'm not it."

"Ah." P.J. nodded once, an exaggerated gesture.

Cade frowned. "What does that mean?"

"The brown-hat syndrome."

"What are you talking about?" he asked.

"You're a bad guy."

He shrugged. "I'm not an ax murderer, if that's what you're saying. I'm just not very good father material. And we don't even want to get into being a husband."

His own father had never missed an opportunity to let him know when a job was less than perfect or his grades not good enough. He figured once a screwup, always a screwup. In everything he tried. That's what made the old man's order for him to go ahead with this summer program such a puzzle. It had obviously meant a lot to his father. He should have entrusted it to someone he had confidence in. Apparently there wasn't anyone else, because he'd dumped it in Cade's lap. If there was any other way to get the ranch, he wouldn't be standing here warning P.J. away.

So he would get through it the best he could; he had no choice but to finish what his father had started. The ranch meant everything to him. He was prepared to do his damnedest to make it a success. If he screwed up, no one could say he hadn't tried. And when his obligation to run this boy's camp was done, the teenagers would leave, along with P.J. and Emily.

He wished it were tomorrow. No way was he the man to do right by any of them. But it was that little girl who worried him the most. She wanted a father. No matter how much he was attracted to her mother, he was the wrong cowboy to try to fill those boots.

"No one is asking you to be a husband," P.J. said, breaking into his thoughts almost as if she could read them.

He heard the words, but he had to make sure she knew he meant what he said. He didn't want her to get hurt.

"Look, P.J., we have to put up with each other until the summer is over. If the next couple months are going to work with those gangster wanna-bes, you and I have to get along."

"I'm not sure what that has to do with anything, but those boys are not even close to outlaws-in-training. Any more than you are," she added with a smile.

That surprised him. Not that she'd stood up for the boys. He'd figured she would do that. In fact he sometimes wondered if he deliberately bad-mouthed them because he liked the way her brown eyes sparkled when she got on her high horse in their defense. He just hadn't been prepared for her to defend him, or to do it with a smile that turned his insides to mush.

"As long as we understand each other," he continued. "Let's put all our cards on the table. If you took this job hoping it would turn into something permanent, you'd best get over the idea. When summer's over, there won't be talk about leading anyone on. I don't want any question about where we stand on this."

Beside her, Lady snorted and P.J. patted her neck. "You're a good girl," she crooned. Then she looked at him and instead of the annoyance or anger he'd expected, she grinned, an expression that lit up her face.

He got the feeling Ms. P. J. Kirkland was laughing at him. "Do we have a deal?" he asked, tamping down his irritation.

"Absolutely," she said. "I couldn't agree with you more. The last thing I want is a husband."

"What about Emily?"

"She's too young for a husband."

He couldn't stop the small smile that tugged at his lips. "That's not what I meant."

"I know. But you walked right into that one, cowboy."

"I'll watch my step from now on. But what about your daughter? She wants a father."

"I'm afraid Em is going to have to learn to be careful what she wishes for."

"How's that?"

"To give her a father, I'd have to take on a husband."

"Take on?"

"I would rather muck out stalls with my bare hands than get married again."

"Why?"

"It's a setup for disappointment. I never planned to do it in the first place. My only excuse is that I was young, inexperienced and vulnerable. David came along and charmed me. If only he'd had more responsibility than charm, we'd have been okay.''

"I'm sure there are guys out there who want to settle down.''

"Then I hope they find someone. It's not me. I did it once, but I'm older and much wiser now. I felt like a yo-yo. I would wind myself up, he would let me down. I psyched myself into believing he would change, he didn't. For a while I kept believing the next time would be different.''

Cade watched her face, the faraway angry look that spread over her features. He wasn't normally given to tuning in to feelings, but somehow he had the notion he was hooked up to P.J.'s frequency. He would swear on his favorite horse that there was more to her hostility than a bad marriage.

"When did you stop?'' he asked.

"Believing things would change?'' When he nodded, she instantly said, "Em's fifth birthday. He promised to take her for a pony ride.''

"What happened?''

"He never showed up and didn't even call. She fell asleep in front of the window watching for him.''

"Son of a b—''

Cade wasn't sure what he'd thought she would say. But somehow hearing the truth was worse. If he ever saw the whites of Kirkland's eyes, the bastard would be sorry. He would teach him the meaning of responsibility.

P.J. looked down and her hair fell around her face like a brown silk curtain. She tucked it behind her ears and looked at him. "Calling him names doesn't help. I tried that. It didn't make me feel even a little bit better. So when he suggested staying away permanently, I shook his hand and said adios.''

"Good for you.''

"I promised myself that she wouldn't be hurt like that again. She's a happy, well-adjusted child. Why would I want to rock the boat?''

"No reason.''

It made perfect sense to him. Cade's own father had been around and had only made him frustrated and angry.

P.J. stroked Lady's neck and he noticed her hand trembled. He wanted to take it between his own, but he didn't dare touch her.

"As a parent, it's my job to prepare Emily for adulthood. I need to teach her that people don't always live up to our expectations. In fact it's probably for the best not to have any, expectations, I mean.''

"I guess.''

Again Cade had the feeling that P.J. was talking about something besides her failed marriage, something that had left a deep scar.

"So you see, even if I were attracted to you, which I'm not,'' she added quickly, "there's no chance that anything could happen. I suspect you have issues from your past to work through. You don't need any distractions. And I will never take a chance with Emily's emotional well-being.''

"Good.''

The word came out automatically. And he was pretty sure he meant it. But he had a gut feeling that P.J. was the pot calling the kettle black. He was no armchair psychologist, but he'd bet she had some issues of her own to work out. What was the term now? Dysfunctional, that was it. Between the two of them, he figured they couldn't function their way out of a paper bag. He was glad they'd had this talk, cleared the air, knew where each of them stood.

She looked straight at him then, and he wasn't sure of anything. Especially not his feelings. Confusion was top of the list. He should be grateful she wasn't attracted to him. But her kiss had said something different.

Cade studied her mouth, tempted to test his theory. He didn't peg her for a game player. She didn't hide her feelings. If he kissed her now would he taste the same fire and wanting as the last time? Should he give her a pop quiz here and now to see if she'd lied?

What good would that do? Stir the pot to overflowing and have nothing but a mess. That's what it would do. Not to mention mixed signals. He had just told her he didn't want anything between them. And she'd agreed, her instinct strong to protect her little girl. He respected that. She was a class-A mother. He was a loner trying to make a go of his life. Their paths would cross for a short time, then they would go in different directions. Kissing her again was the dumbest thing he could do. But as long as she stood there in front of him smelling like flowers and looking like temptation, that's all he could think about.

She patted Lady again and said, "I'd better make sure Em's in bed."

"Yeah."

She brushed past him to the stall's gate and looked back. "You get some sleep. I'll wait up for the boys to get back."

He was glad she'd thought of it. He'd forgotten all about the teenagers at the movies. "Fine."

"Good," she said nodding. "I better go up to the house and make sure my daughter is in bed."

"You just said that."

"Did I?" She looked flustered.

"Yeah." Was she more affected by him than she let on? The idea pleased him.

"Good night, Cade."

"'Night," he answered.

Then she was gone. He should have been relieved. Not even close. His gut told him he should have kissed her. His head said he was a fool. Just like his old man had always told him.

P.J. was right to steer clear of him. He was trouble. But it took one to know one. She was sending out danger signals he would be an idiot to ignore. He planned to spend the rest of the summer avoiding the pretty lady with the warm brown eyes and lips that promised paradise.

A week after "putting their cards on the table" in the barn, P.J. watched Emily wrap up the sandwiches they'd assembled for Cade and the boys. As she supervised her daughter, P.J. made a pitcher of lemonade. She had continued her habit to bring her boss a snack every afternoon and included enough food for the teenagers who were doing their assigned daily chores.

Since their heart-to-heart, Cade never seemed to be around this time of day. She left the food at the barn and when she came back for the dishes, the vittles had disappeared. At first she thought there was an odd job keeping him away. Then she saw a pattern forming. Instinct told her he was deliberately staying out of her way.

Deliberate or not it was probably for the best. On her own, she wasn't sure she was strong enough to resist his temptation. And she couldn't blame it on his charm. The thought made her smile. No one could accuse Cade McKendrick of being overly charming. That's what made his rare flashes of humor more surprising and dear. There was a better word to describe him. Solid. Though he denied it, she sensed dependability in him.

That was a very attractive quality and made her even more sure that the less time they spent together, the better. But she missed their banter. At least *she* bantered; sometimes he zinged her back. If she was lucky, she could coax a smile out of him. Whatever dance they did, she missed it.

"I can't carry all these, Mom." Emily frowned at the pile of sandwiches.

"What I wouldn't give for a chuck wagon," P.J. said ruefully. She put her hands on her hips and surveyed the stack. "I guess we'll just put them in a backpack. Somehow I don't think the guys will mind if they're squished."

"I'm going to carry one for Steve and Mr. Cade so they won't squish," the little girl said.

"That's very sweet of you, Em. I'm sure they'll appreciate it." Although Cade wouldn't know he'd received special treatment because he wouldn't be around. P.J. pulled the canvas backpack from the pantry and they started loading it up.

"Steve likes turkey sandwiches, with mustard. So this one's for him." Emily set it aside. "And Mr. Cade likes baloney."

Not really, P.J. thought. He was a straight shooter. That was the good news. The bad: he was a straight shooter. She almost wished he wasn't. Instead of throwing ice water on her feelings, the talk had been like kerosene on flames. He had been honest. He had told her he wasn't interested in settling down.

Instead of putting her off, that made her like him more. It was tough to resist a man who didn't play games. She could be in for a rough rest of the summer. Except for one thing. The fascination was all on her part. He had flat-out said he wasn't looking for a wife. So she had nothing to worry about.

She tightened the lid on the lemonade container and looked down at her daughter, who held a sandwich in each hand. "Let's go, kidlet."

Emily nodded and they left the kitchen, walking up the slight grade behind the house on their way to the barn. She'd heard Cade say something about showing the boys how to care for the tack. Whatever that meant. She wasn't sure where one worked on tack but figured the barn was a good place to start hunting.

They stopped for a moment so that Emily could inspect the sandwiches she carried and make sure she wasn't squishing them. While she waited, P.J. saw Steve come out of the barn, his movements fast and angry. He was followed by Mark, with Todd bringing up the rear. As they got closer, she could see his face and knew she wasn't wrong about his irritation. But she saw disappointment too.

"Steve, what's the matter?" she asked.

He didn't stop or slow down. "Ask him," he said.

P.J. didn't bother to inquire who "him" was. What had Cade done now? She figured she'd better put on her diplomat hat and get to the bottom of this. It was a good bet Emily shouldn't overhear this conversation. She looked down at her daughter who was staring after the boys. Before she could come up with an alternate plan for her daughter, Em did it for her.

The child handed her the baloney sandwich and held up the other. "I'll take this one to Steve."

P.J. nodded. "If I put the backpack on you, do you think you can handle the food for the other guys too?"

The little girl nodded. "I'm almost eight, Mom. Eight-year-olds are strong."

"Thanks for reminding me. There's more lemonade in the fridge." She arranged the lightweight canvas pack on the child and watched her for a moment as she followed after the boys.

Then P.J. continued on to find Cade and see what had instigated this rebellion in the ranks. Walking into the barn, she was assaulted by the odors of hay and horses. It wasn't an unpleasant smell, and probably seemed stronger as she stood and waited for her eyes to adjust to the dimmer light inside. Toward the rear of the building she heard the rattle of metal on wood and followed the sound. Nearby she found Cade hanging what looked like leather strips from hooks.

Without turning around he said, "You're here to find out what I did to the boys."

Sister Catherine Ilene's favorite platitude popped into her head: A Guilty Conscience Needs No Accuser. Some clichés were so true, she thought wryly.

"Actually I'm here with something for you to eat. It's just a happy coincidence that I can find out why the guys hightailed it out of here. You didn't by any chance suggest they read a romance novel?"

He wasn't even close to smiling when he turned to stare at her. "They wanted to ride the horses and I said no. End of story."

"That went over like a leaky rowboat."

"Yeah. Actually Mark and Todd took it okay. Steve went ballistic."

"Do you blame him, Cade?"

"You bet I do."

"Did you think about the fact that he's been here a couple weeks now. He hasn't asked for anything—except to ride. You keep telling him no."

"I'm not a hotshot English teacher like you, but last time I checked, 'no' was a complete sentence."

She ignored his sarcasm. "What if you were in his shoes, or boots as the case may be?" Still holding his baloney sandwich, she shook it at him. "What would you do? Smile and say mucking out stalls is almost as good as riding a horse?"

"He's too unpredictable. That hair-trigger temper is a setup for disaster. How can I trust him to be disciplined with a horse?"

P.J. thought for a minute. She never saw the side of Steve that Cade was describing. Maybe because most of the time he was with her, Emily was with them. "He's wonderful with my daughter. I've never heard him raise his voice or be less than gentle with her. Even when she wants him to roughhouse, he won't."

"Is she with him now?"

"Probably. I sent her after the guys with the sandwiches we made to hold them over till dinner."

Cade ran his hand over the tack in a gesture that looked like he was checking for tangles. Or running his fingers through a woman's hair. She pushed that thought away quick. Concentrate, she scolded herself.

"Mark and Todd are good kids," he said. "I wouldn't worry about them."

"I agree."

"But Steve is trouble. Keep Emily away from him."

"I disagree. But thanks for caring about Em. I'm touched at your concern."

"Don't blow me off, P.J. He's trouble. Takes one to know one."

"You're saying I should be afraid of you?"

"Yeah."

"So that's why you've been avoiding me?"

He looked startled for a second, then ignored her question. "I've noticed the way Emily follows him around. He's an accident looking for a place to happen. I don't want her near him when it does."

"I thought you said you don't know anything about being a father."

"Who says I do?" he countered.

"I don't know if I'd put a label on it, but your paternal instincts with Emily are on high beam. So why do you turn it off with Steve? He's a kid too. Is it too much like looking in the mirror?"

He whirled to face her, blue eyes blazing. "Stick with English, teach," he said, his voice cool. "Psychology isn't your specialty."

"I nailed you didn't I?" She stood her ground, folding her arms over her chest. "You see a lot of yourself in Steve and you don't much like it."

"Look, they're not ready to ride. End of conversation."

"Not so fast, cowboy. How are they going to get ready if you keep brushing them off? Work with them."

"It's not that simple," he said.

"Yes, it is."

"I don't—"

"Have time. Yeah. Right." She was losing her temper. She just hoped it didn't cause her to lose her job. But holding her tongue wasn't her strong suit. "You're avoiding them. That's the short answer. They know it and are reacting to it."

"You don't always get what you want in life."

She guessed he'd heard that platitude a time or two. Probably from his father. Maybe it was time to butt heads with clichés. "That's true. And a useful lesson when we want something beyond our reach. But in this case, what they want is within your power to give them. Get them ready."

"It takes time—"

"Make time."

A muscle in his cheek contracted, but when he spoke his voice was level and cold as ice. "I can't."

"You mean you won't. Worse, you don't want to." She shook her head and started to walk away. The words were dammed up inside her and she couldn't hold them back, not even if he told her to get out of Dodge. "You were right."

"That's a switch. You keep telling me I'm wrong."

"Not about being good father material." She let out a long breath. "It doesn't take sophisticated training or a genetic predisposition to be a good dad. You just need to *be there* with the desire to do the best you can. You refuse to do either. All you can think about is the ranch."

"It's the only thing that never let me down."

"Did you ever give anyone else a chance?"

"Of course I did."

"As an adult? You said yourself that you and your

father hadn't spoken much since you left home at eighteen. You weren't much older then than Steve is now. You were just a kid. When you grew up did you even try to understand him?''

"It's best to forget that. The probation officer and rep from social services thought everything was fine when they checked us out last week. Leave it alone P.J.''

"Have you ever heard the expression no pain, no gain?''

"Are we back to amateur psychology again?''

He shut her down tighter than the mall on Christmas day. There was no point in wasting any more time and energy trying to convince him otherwise. "It's your loss, cowboy.''

She walked out of the barn and tried to decide if she should start dinner or start packing.

Chapter Five

Cade continued to brush his horse with short, firm strokes long after he'd wiped away the sweat from his ride. It was the least he could do after pushing the animal the way he had. The last time he'd done that, he'd been seventeen-years-old and his father had just brought him home after his brief encounter with the law. He'd been grounded, trapped like a caged tiger. Cade was certain his old man had no idea what he was feeling. On top of that, no way did anyone, not even his father, have the right to tell him what to do. Cade McKendrick was a man. So he'd left the prison of his room and rode for hours. On his father's horse, the most ornery mount on the ranch.

Every ounce of his concentration had been focused on staying in the saddle. He'd had no time to think about anything but survival. He thought his father hadn't even known he was gone. Not till he'd been called home when Matt McKendrick took sick. He'd brought up the incident and let Cade know he hadn't been fooled.

After Cade's talk with P.J. earlier he'd needed to clear his mind, push her out. His run-in with the law had been a cakewalk compared to dealing with P. J. Kirkland. What right did she have to preach? He didn't owe these kids anything. They could spend the summer on the ranch, that didn't mean he had to waste precious work time with them. But he kept galloping toward the same fence with no way to clear it.

The boys were restless. They needed input from him or the program would fail. If he didn't hold up his end of the bargain and see the three boys his father had handpicked through the summer, he could kiss the ranch goodbye.

He patted Midnight's gleaming black neck one last time and was just about to leave the stall when he heard a noise in another part of the barn. One of the horses snorted and pawed restlessly. Was someone in there? It was nearly dark. The hands were in the bunkhouse eating supper. P.J. would have the kids with her. Who else could be in here?

Just then he heard a frightened cry and a thump. It sounded like Emily. His chest tightened with fear. Quickly closing the stall gate, he hurried toward the sound. It seemed like forever, but couldn't have taken him more than a couple seconds until he saw the open gate and Emily sprawled in the hay.

Steve stood next to the black-and-white horse holding a saddle in his hands. Didn't take a mental giant to figure out what he was up to.

Cade shot him a deadly look, then knelt next to a whimpering Emily. She was chalky-white and her eyes were frantic. She'd probably had the wind knocked out of her.

He brushed the hair back from her forehead. "Relax, Emily. In a few seconds you'll catch your breath. Do you hurt anywhere?"

She shook her head, but he checked her arms and legs. Serious injury didn't always cause pain right away. When it didn't appear that anything was broken, his heartbeat slowed to something resembling normal. He lifted her and rested her shoulders against his bent knee so that she could breathe easier.

Then he glared at the teenager. "Get the hell out of here before I do something I'll regret."

"I just wanted to ride. I didn't know—"

"Spare me the lame excuses."

"But I didn't know she was there. When I did, I told her to go back to the house," he said, a desperate note in his voice. "Is she okay?"

Cade held up his hand. He didn't buy the repentant act. "I said get out of my sight. I don't want to look at you."

"No kidding." The words dripped sarcasm. Fear, regret, then anger flickered over the boy's face.

Cade recognized every emotion because he'd felt them all at the hands of his father. Sympathy started to creep in, but he pushed it away as he looked down at Emily. His hands curled into fists. Steve broke the rules. That was bad enough. Endangering this little girl was the last straw. He'd tried to warn P.J. that the teenager was trouble. He'd tried to tell her to keep Emily away from him or she would get hurt. As he glanced at the little girl's white-as-chalk, frightened face he took no satisfaction in being right.

He looked at Steve again. "I told you to leave. Do it," he hollered.

He felt Emily flinch as Steve dropped the saddle and ran from the barn. "It's okay, honey. You're fine."

"Steve," she gasped. "Where's he—"

"Don't worry about him." Cade lifted her into his arms. "I'm going to take you to your mom."

"No." But she put her arms around his neck. "Gotta find Steve."

He walked out of the barn and headed up to the house with her. "Stay away from him, Emily."

"No. You hurt his feelings. I just gotta talk to him."

Exasperated, Cade shook his head. Miss Goody Two-Shoes in training. Like mother, like daughter. If they weren't careful, they were going to get their hearts broken. But it wasn't his job to protect them. He kept walking toward the house, anxious to give Emily back to her mother.

"Kids don't know what's best," he told her.

Those words produced a very weird feeling in the pit of his stomach. Then a sort of déjà vu sensation washed over him. How many times had his father said that to him? Or this hurts me more than it does you?

"Grown-ups don't know everything," the child answered, sticking her lip out. "My mom says so."

He had the feeling he'd flunked another one of Emily's tests. Had his father felt this same sense of failure with him? It was only a failure if you wanted to pass. Cade hadn't wanted any part of the kids, the camp, or anything else the old man had started.

Emily was wrong about grown-ups, at least in his father's case. He'd had all the answers. He'd always known what he was doing. He never failed. But the more Cade was around P.J. and her daughter, the more he felt his inadequacy. Every time he turned around, he let them down.

P.J. had told him being there was the most important part of fatherhood. He wasn't convinced. His father had always been there for him, and had raised a son who was nothing to write home about. But he remembered the passion in her voice when she'd said it, and her emphasis on the words. Someone hadn't been there for her. He knew it as surely as he knew the little girl he carried was wiggling to be free.

He mounted the front steps, unwilling to put her anywhere but safely in her mother's arms. As he walked through the front door, P.J. was right there looking worried. As soon as she saw the child in his arms, her mouth curved up in a smile. It was like the sun coming out of the clouds on a stormy day.

"You found her," she said.

"I wasn't exactly looking," he answered. "She sort of dropped in."

Emily giggled, letting her pout go as she tightened her hold on his neck.

"What happened?" P.J. asked. "Why are you carrying her? Is she all right?"

"I'm fine, Mommy. I fell into the hay."

A thorough maternal onceover seemed to reassure her. She nodded with satisfaction. "That's one accounted for. We still can't find Steve."

The kid had had plenty of time to beat them back to the house. Cade didn't want to feel concern, but he did. "Are you sure he isn't upstairs?"

P.J. shook her head. "We missed him and Emily a little while ago and I fanned out the posse to search.

He couldn't have gotten in without someone seeing him. What happened?'' she asked again.

"He was trying to saddle one of the horses.''

"Did you tell him he could?''

"Of course not.'' Cade shook his head. "It's lucky that I happened to be in the barn to stop him.''

"Why were you? It's getting late.''

He didn't want to explain that thoughts of her had made him restless, so he ignored the question. "I told you to keep Emily away from him. That she was going to get hurt. She fell from the stall fence. The horse was nervous with strangers and all. Emily could have been badly hurt or worse. When I get my hands on that kid—'' He was on a roll and couldn't seem to stop. "It was stupid to take that little girl with him. I can believe he would disregard my rules, but this harebrained scheme—''

A small hand insistently patting his shoulder stopped him. He'd almost forgotten he was still holding Emily. Glancing into her green eyes, he saw the worried frown that puckered her forehead.

"It's not his fault, Mr. Cade. That's what I been tryin' t'tell you. I just went. He told me to g-go away. He said both of us shouldn't get into hot water. What does that mean?'' She sniffled and rubbed a grubby hand beneath her nose. "Don't be mad at Steve. Is he still in trouble?''

P.J. took the little girl from him. "I don't know about him, young lady, but you've definitely earned a time-out.''

"We just wanted to r-ride the horse,'' she said, clutching her mother's neck. "Mr. Cade yelled awful loud. I thought Steve was gonna cry.''

"You came down on Steve pretty hard?" P.J. asked.

"Yeah."

Two pairs of eyes, both concerned, stared at him. Definitely double trouble. And that was putting it mildly. Cade shuffled his feet, uncomfortable with the mother/daughter scrutiny. They made him feel like he'd drop-kicked a puppy. But, damn it, riding without permission or supervision or even a little training was a serious offense. Still, Cade knew he could probably have dealt more calmly if Emily hadn't been involved. It was Steve's blatant disregard for the child's safety that had put him over the edge. Now he knew Steve hadn't invited her along.

"You have to find him," P.J. said.

"And tell him what?"

"That you were wrong."

She was reading his mind again, Cade thought irritably. Without waiting for him to say anything, she continued, "You assumed that he had included Emily in his clandestine scheme. I know he has to suffer the consequences of breaking the rules, but it's not as bad as it first seemed. What matters now is finding him."

"He'll come back when he's ready."

"What if he doesn't? Besides, it's getting dark. We don't know how far he went. What if he gets lost? What if there are grizzlies, mountain lions or coyotes?"

"Or snakes?" Emily added, eyes wide and frightened.

P.J. clutched her daughter tighter. "What if—"

He held up his hand. "All right. I'll find him."

As he started to turn away, Emily wiggled and her

mother set her down. She grabbed his hand. "Can I go with you?"

This was another test. He could feel it. Knowing he was going to flunk, he said, "Sorry half-pint. It will be faster if I go by myself." When her lip began to quiver, he felt like the slime on the underside of a river-bottom rock. He hunched down to her level. "You want me to find Steve, don't you?"

She nodded reluctantly.

"Then I need to go as fast as I can."

"You're absolutely right." P.J. smiled and nodded approvingly.

Cade blinked. He'd passed, at least the maternal test. How about that? It felt pretty darn good. He looked into big brown eyes that still showed traces of worry. And something else. It took him a minute, but he recognized trust in her expression. Confidence in his ability to find the missing teenager and bring him back safely. She didn't doubt him. That made him want to justify her faith in him.

"I'll find him. Don't worry."

"Back in the saddle again," Cade mumbled as he swung up on his horse.

He decided that would be the fastest way to find the runaway teen. A full moon gave him enough light and it would be the best way to cover ground quickly. He figured the boy couldn't have gone far on foot. But there were a lot of places to hide if he didn't want to be found. Cade knew a good number of those places.

Surprisingly, it didn't take him long to find Steve. Cade spotted him at the top of a rise about a mile from the house. He was silhouetted against the moon,

as he sat on a rock. Cade stopped his mount and slid
out of the saddle. He held the reins in his hand as he
approached the brooding boy.

He stood there for a few moments and neither of
them spoke. Finally he said, "Emily told me she followed you. She said you told her to go back to the
house."

In the moonlight he could read the hostile stare
Steve shot him. "So you believe *her*."

"Let's not argue about it. P.J. and Emily are worried about you."

"I'm okay. I can take care of myself."

"Yeah. Let's go on back to the house so they don't
worry any longer than they have to."

"What about what I did? I mean trying to ride the
horse?"

"You were wrong. Everyone's entitled to a mistake. I'll give you one more chance."

"Big wow."

"It's getting late. I'm hungry and tired. You don't
want to tweak my tail right now, son."

"Dude, don't call me son."

"Okay. If you don't call me dude." He wasn't sure
but he thought the boy's mouth quirked upward in a
quick grin.

"Deal, d—" He stopped and looked as if he
wanted to ask something.

"You can call me Cade."

"Okay."

Cade put his left boot in the stirrup and swung back
into the saddle. Steve started to walk ahead of him.

"Want a lift?" he asked the teen.

The boy glanced over his shoulder and in the
moonlight Cade could read his surprise.

Then the shutter fell. "Nah. I'll walk."

The kid was practicing self-preservation. Never let anyone see what you really want. They'll snatch it right out of your grasp. But his yearning to ride was what had gotten him into this mess in the first place. Cade figured he had to shoulder some of the blame. He understood better than anyone the benefits of a hard ride. Hadn't he done that earlier to shake off the unsettling effect one Ms. P. J. Kirkland had on him? Luckily no real harm had been done.

Cade stopped the horse beside him. "Like I said, it's late, I'm hungry and tired. If I come in without you, P.J. and Emily will have my hide. This is the fastest way." He held out his hand. After a moment's hesitation, Steve took it and Cade said, "Put your foot in the stirrup and swing up behind me."

Steve grudgingly did as he was told. But Cade was almost sure he saw a wide grin on the kid's face just before he ducked his head. He felt like grinning himself.

P.J. watched the three boys and Emily play Scrabble at the dining-room table. Cade was upstairs showering before he came down to the dinner she'd kept warm for him. She was dying to hear what had happened when he'd found Steve. Although he'd looked tired, she'd sensed an easing of tension between them. That was a relief. Otherwise the rest of the summer would have been pretty miserable.

When she finally heard Cade's door shut, and his tread on the stairs, she went into the kitchen to make sure the pot roast, mashed potatoes and vegetables on the warming tray were hot enough. Without turning around, she knew when he'd entered the room. The unique scent of him, shampoo, soap, and aftershave, clued her in to his presence. It was like a one-two punch. He came in a room, the fluttery feeling in her stomach commenced. It felt like all the nerve endings in her body went on high alert.

"Would you like some coffee?" she asked without turning around. Why intensify the sensation by looking at him? She might maintain a semblance of dignity if she deprived one of her senses.

"Yeah." With a weary sigh, he sat down at the table. "How did you know?"

She put the plate of food in front of him. "You look like you've been rode hard and put away wet."

He smiled. "You're really getting into the lingo."

"I've seen my share of westerns."

"I hear an 'and' coming."

She glanced over her shoulder as she pulled a mug from the cupboard. "And they're not much like a real working ranch." She smiled as she poured him a cup of coffee. "But it's fun to talk like that."

He looked up at her as she put the steaming mug in front of him. "Thanks."

"You're welcome."

He started eating and after a few bites, met her gaze. "Thanks for this, too. It's mighty tasty, ma'am."

"Thank you, kind sir." She grinned. He was definitely loosening up. Maybe this would be as good a time as any to ask him. "What happened with you and Steve?"

"I told him Emily confirmed his story, then offered him a lift back."

She had a suspicion there was more to it than that, but he was a man. She wasn't likely to get details.

And there was something else that had been on her mind. "Cade?"

"Hmm?" He scooped up a forkful of food and shoveled it in.

"How did you get to Emily so fast when she fell?"

His fork stopped halfway between mouth and mashed potatoes. He shot her an almost guilty look. "I just happened to be in the barn."

"Why? Steve isn't stupid. He wouldn't have tried to get away with something if he thought you would be there."

"Like you said. This is a working ranch. I was working."

"But it was late. Even for you."

He bent his head and continued eating. Between bites he said, "I'd just finished brushing down my horse."

"So you were riding until nearly sundown. Was there something special you were doing?"

He shrugged, a little too casually. "Checking fences. General look-see."

"Oh."

"I heard a question in that one word. Spit it out."

"How about oh, you missed dinner and didn't have the decency to call?"

He glanced up quickly and visibly relaxed the tension in his shoulders when he saw her smile. One corner of his mouth quirked up. "There aren't a lot of phones out on the range."

"A likely story," she said.

"I reckon I'll have to take you out and show you."

"And just how would we get there? Truck? Wagon? Helicopter?"

"Well it begins with 'h,' but it's got four legs and

rumor has it you've never been within spitting distance of one.''

"My mama didn't raise fools. You're talking about horseback.''

"You got it.''

"Steve might go out on a limb to ride a horse. But this little lady likes two feet on the ground and animals small enough to see the tops of their heads.''

"You don't know what you're missing.''

"At least it wasn't dinner. Like you.''

"You're not about to let loose of that any time soon, are you?''

"Sure. As soon as you fess up to what you were really doing out there.''

If she were a betting woman, she'd wager that spur-of-the-moment tour had something to do with her. She knew he hadn't planned to work late. Normally he let her know when he wouldn't be there for a meal. Today he hadn't. She couldn't shake the feeling that his ride had something to do with their conversation earlier in the afternoon. Well, maybe conversation was too glorified a word. She'd given him a piece of her mind. He'd listened. Then she'd left in a bit of a huff. Well, a lot of a huff.

He broke open one of the biscuits she'd set in front of him, then buttered it. Finally he met her gaze. "I took a ride to clear my head. Happy now?''

"Not especially. I figure I drove you to that because I was an overbearing, preachy witch. This is your home. I had no right. I apologize.''

"Forget it.''

"I promise it won't happen again.''

He set his fork on his cleaned plate and gave her

a doubtful look. "Yeah. And in July we'll be shoveling snow instead of horse—"

Shouts of laughter drifted in from the dining room. She walked the couple steps to the doorway. "Everything all right in here?"

Emily looked at her from where she sat on Steve's lap. "We're winning, Mom."

"Good for you. But is it fair you two ganging up on Mark and Todd?" She winked at the other boys.

Todd grinned. "Steve needs her help. Otherwise we'd win too easy."

P.J. nodded, then turned back to Cade. For a moment, she thought there was a wistful look in his blue eyes. Then the expression was gone.

She sat down across from him. "You don't think I can keep my nose out of things?"

"What?"

"Your sarcastic reference to snow in July implies that you think I can't keep my two cents to myself."

"You said it. Not me." He raised one eyebrow. "And how do you do that?"

"What did I do now?"

"Go from one conversation to another and keep them both straight."

"I'm a woman."

"There's a news flash." He was staring at her mouth when he said that. The look on his face caused her idling pulse to go off the scale in zero point three seconds.

Raised voices in the other room interrupted the moment. There was a good-natured, but heated disagreement over a word.

"P.J.?" It was Mark.

"I'm being paged." She rose and went to the doorway. "What?"

"You're an English teacher, right?"

"That's the rumor."

"Is 'zorax' a word?"

She laughed. "You should know better than to ask a teacher to do the work for you." She glanced over her shoulder, immensely gratified when she noticed Cade taking a second helping of all the food she'd made. "Do you have a dictionary around these parts, cowboy? There seems to be a shootout brewing."

"In the office," he answered.

She looked at the kids around the table. "Last time I played this game, you had to go out on a limb and challenge any word you think is wrong. Are you willing to do that?" she asked Mark.

"Do you know the answer?" he shot back to her.

"Yes. But it would be cheating if I told you."

"But Steve's trying to jack up his points by using a Z and an X on a triple-word-score square."

"He's pretty smart," P.J. said.

"Does that mean it's a word?"

All the kids looked at her with great interest. "I already told you it would be cheating for me to get involved. You have to decide whether or not to trust your instincts."

Steve grinned at his friend. "I wouldn't, bro. A zorax is that thing in your throat that connects to your lungs. Remember we learned about it in biology." He shot P.J. a look and there was a twinkle in his eyes.

"We didn't study anything like that," Mark answered, looking unsure. He looked past her to Cade. "What do you think? Is it a word?"

She felt the heat of his body as he stood behind

her. "I think P.J. is right. You guys should figure it out."

Mark turned his ever-present baseball hat so that the bill covered his neck. "Can't you even give us a hint?"

"That would be taking the easy way out, son." Cade exchanged a look with Steve.

"Mr. Cade?" Emily leaned forward and knocked the letter tiles off the stand.

"What?" he said.

"Why don't you eat in the dining room with us? When you're done, we can start a new game and all play."

Although not quite touching him, P.J. felt Cade stiffen.

"Not tonight, Emily," he finally answered.

P.J. knew he'd gone back to the kitchen table before the disappointed look settled on her daughter's face. She had seen that expression more times than she could count, and every time her heart broke for her little girl. "Tell you what. When this round is over, I challenge you to a game. Loser does dishes for a week."

"Can we play teams?" Mark asked. "After all, you're an English teacher and everything."

"I'll take on all four of you," she said.

The boys nodded agreement and started their male bragging rituals. She turned back into the kitchen and sat down across from Cade. Since she'd just promised to stop preaching, she chose something harmless to say.

"I didn't expect them to have this much fun with that game. Are you sure you don't want to join them?"

"I'm sure."

"I found it in the office." She folded her hands and rested them on the table. "Did you play with your father?"

He laughed bitterly. "Matt McKendrick didn't have time for games." He rose and took his empty plate to the sink, washed it off and put it in the dishwasher.

"I could have done that," she said. "It's my job."

He glanced into the dining room where the kids were laughing and trading verbal barbs. "They need you. Why don't you go referee."

Without another word, he walked outside.

Chapter Six

Cade folded his arms over his chest and stared into the yard. Moonlight bathed the grass and walkway in an eerie glow. A while ago he'd felt a rare sense of satisfaction, when he'd brought Steve back. P.J.'s pleased expression and a hearty hug from Emily had made him feel like he'd done something good, something worthwhile. Something he wished his father could have seen. Maybe it would have canceled out his car-stealing escapade.

The door opened behind him and as the scent of flowers surrounded him, he knew who was there. P.J. moved beside him and rested one curvy hip on the porch railing. She breathed deeply and sighed. "Smell the jasmine. It's like Mother Nature's perfume."

If only it was strong enough to cover the sweet, sexy, womanly scent of her, he thought. But all he said was, "Yeah."

"I'd like to plant some in my garden at home,"

she continued. "It's so sweet, so fragrant, aromatic, ambrosial, so—"

"Stop." He repressed his gut-clenching reaction to her reference of home, a reminder that she was leaving at the end of the summer. Instead he shot her a wry glance. "Practicing?"

"For what?" she asked, meeting his gaze.

"Flexing your vocabulary muscles. For the upcoming Scrabble competition."

"Oh. Not really." She took another deep breath as she imitated his stance and folded her arms over her chest. "It just smells so wonderful, I got carried away."

The simple things in life were enough for Miss Goody Two-Shoes. He wished it were that easy for him. "If you're finished sniffing, there's a room full of kids just dying to take you apart at word games."

"Yeah. I could use some help, cowboy."

He shook his head. "You don't need me."

"What's wrong, Cade?" She put her hand on his arm. "Please don't tell me nothing. I'm not an idiot. There's something bothering you. And don't give me some hooey about dabbling in psychology. It doesn't take a shrink's training to see when a friend is troubled."

Friends? Is that what they were? He stared down at her. She looked beautiful in the moonlight, or any light, he thought. Strands of dark hair rested on her shoulders. Her brown eyes grew big with concern. For him, he guessed, since there was no one else around.

He couldn't remember the last time, if ever, a woman had truly cared that he was troubled. He wanted to kiss her again. Every time he saw her the urge grew stronger to see if that first kiss was a fluke, or if the heart-pumping and blood-pressure raising would happen again. Had she forgotten about it? She'd said she would. And she'd just now called him a friend. Was it normal for a friend to think about kissing his friend senseless?

"Cade?"

"Hmm?"

"Tell me what you're thinking."

He laughed. "Trust me. You don't want to go there."

"Then tell me why you walked out so abruptly just now."

He sighed. "How do you make it look so easy, P.J.?"

She tilted her head to the side, obviously taken aback by his question. "What?" she asked, shrugging.

"This." He held his arm out, indicating the house, and the group of young people visible through the dining room window.

"You're going to have to be just a hair more specific. I'd like to know what I'm taking credit for."

"In a mere five weeks, you've turned this house into a home."

"It was a home when I got here."

He shook his head. "Nope. Not even close. I lived in that," he hesitated a moment searching for the right word. "Building," he finally said. "I spent eighteen years here and it never felt as much like a home as you've made it in such a short time. How do you do it?"

Shyly, she cast her gaze down and self-consciously rocked back on her heels. "I'm flattered that you think I've done something, but truly I don't know what."

Maybe it was just *her,* the special person she was, that had made the difference. She didn't have to do anything specific. She just had to be there. He remembered her comment about fathers not having to do anything in particular. Being around was half the battle. Could it really be that easy?

"You've made a family of sorts out of that motley group," he said, angling his head toward the kids.

"I notice you didn't say 'us.' You refuse to include yourself. What about you, Cade?"

He shrugged. "I'm just the boss. I don't fit in any better now than when I was a teenager. How can you waltz in here and pull everything together?"

She stared up at him. "I suppose it's just because I'm a woman."

She'd meant the remark in the most innocent way. But the feelings it generated in him went from touch-and-go to downright dangerous. He looked into her eyes and let his gaze roam freely over her full lips, then lower to her rounded breasts temptingly outlined by the yellow T-shirt she wore, and lower still to her curvy hips and shapely legs encased in soft, worn denim. As much as he'd like to forget the fact, she was definitely all-woman.

"I'm not sure I get your drift," he finally said, annoyed that his voice cracked a little.

"It's easier for women. We're naturally nesters. We pull in a bit of this, a smidgen of that and," she threw her arm out in a circular motion, "Voilà. A building becomes a home. Nesting." Her brow puckered thoughtfully.

"What about your mother? You've never mentioned her."

He shrugged. "Never knew her. She died when I was two or three. Car accident."

"I'm so sorry," she said. "But it explains a lot."

"About why I'm nesting impaired?"

"You're joking. But if you hadn't provided the nest, none of us would be here. Those boys, desperate for attention and affection, wouldn't have the opportunity to see that home can be a haven."

Those boys aren't the only ones, he thought. This place was more welcoming than he'd ever seen it. He almost wished he belonged with them. Then he reminded himself that it was temporary. When she left at the end of the summer, the nest would go back to being just bits of this and that with no one to breathe life and vitality and warmth into it.

"You make it look easy," he said again.

"Attitude."

"What?"

"It's all in your attitude. You can peek through the window, or you can march right in and participate. Let the chips fall where they may. Stragglers get left behind." She glanced up at him quickly. "Did that sound preachy? I didn't mean it to and that wasn't a lecture aimed at you." She held her hand up in a solemn gesture. "I swear it wasn't."

He grinned. "I guess you can take the teacher out of the classroom. But you can't take the classroom out of the teacher."

"I'm sorry, Cade. You should just tell me to zip it before I get started."

"What you said makes a lot of sense. But why

should I march right in? I don't have anything to give."

Quickly, she turned her body to face him, unconsciously stepping closer. "Oh, but you do," she said earnestly. "There's so much you could show them. You don't even have to do that. Just let them hang around you. Be a role model."

"Oh, no," he said, shaking his head. "No way. I'm the wrong one for them to look up to."

"I don't know why you deny the fact that you're a good man," she said, putting her hand on his arm.

Her touch sent sparks arcing through him. The evening air was pleasantly cool, but his skin felt hot. Before he knew what he was doing, he encircled her waist with his arm and pulled her close. Then he lowered his mouth to hers. He tasted surprise on her lips, then she went soft all over and molded her body to his. She fit him perfectly. Slipping his hand into the silken threads of her hair, he gently pressed the back of her head, making the contact of their mouths more firm.

When she sighed, her sweet breath fanned the embers of desire glowing inside him. He traced the outline of her lips with his tongue, then slid inside to sample the waiting, welcoming warmth.

This is where I belong.

The thought was reinforced when P.J. slid her arm up over his shoulder and curved her hand around his neck. The breath caught in his throat. His heart thundered like the ground beneath the hooves of a runaway horse. Her breasts, flattened against his chest, making him feel like he'd died and gone to heaven. He was about to deepen the kiss when the front door opened.

"Mommy?"

In half a heartbeat they were a foot apart.

"W-what is it, Em?" P.J. asked, touching her mouth with a trembling hand.

Cade heard the tremor in her voice. He couldn't stop his surge of satisfaction. He wasn't the only one affected by that kiss.

"The game is over, Mommy. It's your turn to play."

"Okay. Tell the boys I'll be right there." As the door closed, she let out a long breath. Warily, she looked up at him. "Are you going to tell me to forget that kiss too?"

"Nope."

"Good thing. I'd tell you what you want to hear. But I'm afraid it would be a lie."

He smiled at her back as she went inside. Who'd have guessed Miss Goody Two-Shoes was a fibber? Or that he'd be grinning like a fool because she was?

"Emily?" P.J. walked through the barn, feeling her anxiety intensify with each step.

Only last night they'd dealt with a teenage crisis and today things had seemed surprisingly normal. But maybe she'd jumped to that conclusion too soon.

She hadn't seen her little girl for a long time. After lunch, she'd been baking dessert for that night when Emily had raced into the house. What P.J. had understood from the breathless words pouring out of her was that Cade had sent her to ask permission to be in the corral. As long as he was with Em, P.J. said permission granted. But that was hours ago. She'd expected to see her child long before this.

"Emily? Where are you?" she called, stopping

momentarily to listen for an answer. To her frustration, there wasn't one.

She started walking again, increasing her pace. As she passed the stalls, she noted that they were empty except for one or two. Odd, she thought. She knew the horses were exercised regularly, but not usually so many at the same time. As she moved from the dim interior of the barn to the corral beyond, it took a moment for her eyes to adjust to the sunlight.

When she could see clearly, she blinked several times to make sure she wasn't imagining the scene. The three teenage boys and her daughter were on horseback, walking in a circle around the picket-fenced enclosure. Cade was there protectively close to Emily who was mounted on Lady. P.J. had never before seen such a look of happiness on her daughter's face. A lump of maternal emotion formed in her throat.

Mark, Todd and Steve seemed to be having fun too. She knew it wasn't cool for them to let on that they were. But she didn't miss the excitement sparkling in their eyes.

Emily spotted her. "Hi, Mommy."

"Hi yourself, kidlet," she said. The boys waved and called out greetings, then returned their concentration to guiding their horses.

Cade put a hand on Lady's neck. "Do you remember how I told you to stop her?" he asked Emily. She nodded and pulled back gently on the reins she carefully held in her left hand. The animal halted.

"Good girl," he said to a beaming Emily.

P.J. moved next to him and looked up at her daughter.

"Mommy," she said, her whole body seeming to

hum with excitement. "Cade introduced Steve and Mark and Todd to their horses just like he did me and Lady. He showed us how to brush them and how to use the hoof pick and how to take care of them. He taught us about putting the bridle over their ears. He wouldn't let me put the saddle on 'cuz I'm not tall enough yet, but he let me make sure the blanket was smooth and comfortable before the boys did. He says we're ready for the trail. He says—"

"Whoa, kidlet. Take a breath before we have to call a code blue." She met the gaze of Emily's hero.

Frowning, Cade returned her look. "You worried?"

"Yeah. At least I was," she amended.

"You're not now?"

She rubbed her forehead. "If it looks that way, you can chalk it up to age. As the years pile on, it takes longer for the worry lines to disappear."

"Why were you concerned?"

"I hadn't seen Em for way too long. She said she'd be in the corral with you, but it took some time to find her because this is the last place I looked. I figured you'd be finished with whatever you were doing by now."

"Didn't she ask you if she could have a riding lesson?"

P.J. followed his glance up to the little girl who seemed overly fascinated by an ordinary, cloudless blue sky.

"Emily?" he said with just the right note of censure in his deep voice.

"I told Mommy I was going to the corral and she said it was okay if you were there," her daughter said meekly.

Cade swung his glance back to her. "She didn't tell you she would be on a horse?" When P.J. shook her head, he continued, "I'm sorry. I wouldn't have let her if I'd known."

He started to lift Em down and P.J. stopped him with a hand on his arm. Quickly, she drew her arm back and took a step away.

"It's okay. The look on her face when she was riding—" The lump in her throat reappeared and blocked the words. She put a hand over her mouth and turned away embarrassed at the emotion she couldn't suppress.

"I think that's enough for today," Cade said to the kids.

"Aw, gee." That was Todd. "We were just getting good."

"Yeah," Mark chimed in. "Can't we keep going? Maybe even somewhere besides in a circle?"

"A trail ride?" Steve added. "That would be so awesome."

"Tomorrow we'll do some more practicing. If you don't get off soon, your backside won't be in any condition for a merry-go-round ride," Cade said.

"You mean we really get to do this again?" Steve asked. Excitement and amazement twisted together in his voice.

"Yup."

Even with her back turned to him, P.J. knew that was Cade's voice. The lack of verbiage was a huge clue, but it was the deep, sexy timbre raising goose bumps on her skin that left no doubt.

"You guys dismount and walk your horses back to their stalls." Leather creaked, and when he said,

"You too, buckaroo," P.J. turned to watch him lift Emily down.

"Steve?" Cade looked at the tallest of the young men.

"Yeah?" The teenager in question stopped as the other two, with their horses in tow, disappeared into the barn.

Cade walked over to him and handed him Lady's reins. "Would you mind helping Emily with the saddle and make sure she brushes the animal the way I showed all of you?"

Steve nodded. "Sure thing."

Cade clapped him on the shoulder. "Thanks."

"C'mon, Em 'n' Em," the teen said.

Emily giggled. "Will you let me take off the saddle?" she asked Steve.

"Maybe the blanket," he said leading the two horses into the barn.

His back to her, Cade watched until they had gone, then stood listening for a few moments. Thank goodness. She needed more than a few moments to compose herself.

Oh, man. *Penelope Jane Kirkland, you are in a lot of trouble.*

Not only because he had kissed her last night. At least he hadn't made her promise to forget it. She'd hardly been able to think about anything else. Meals had been pretty basic. She was so preoccupied by Cade's kiss, elaborate food preparation was risking another kitchen fire.

Mostly she was in deep water because Cade was changing his attitude. Participating. Getting involved. He had actually *listened* to her. After weeks of her preaching, he had actually spent time with the kids teaching them about horses. It wasn't bad enough that his rugged cowboy good looks did sinful things to her insides. And his kisses were to die for. But he had to be a nice guy too. The triple whammy. How was she supposed to resist him?

She had to find a way.

A fatherless childhood had taught her that men don't stick around for the long haul. After that, the only time she hadn't left a relationship first, she'd been charmed into letting her guard down and getting married. Disaster quickly followed. Worst of all, it wasn't just her suffering the consequences. Em had paid a high price too. She wouldn't make the same mistake. She couldn't ask her daughter to pay again. She couldn't count on anyone but herself.

She settled her gaze on the collar of Cade's plaid work shirt, then lowered it to his broad shoulders, and finally to his backside encased in saddle-smoothed denim. Swallowing hard, she knew she had to fight her attraction with every ounce of energy she could muster. The first weapon at her disposal was playing it cool. She must never, ever let him kiss her again. Why had she let him in the first place?

He turned around and flashed her his hunk-and-a-half grin. 'Nuff said. That look melted her defenses faster than an ice cube in a microwave. Not only that, there was a predatory glitter in his blue eyes that stole the breath from her lungs. Her heart turned over in her chest and her legs wobbled like pillars in an earthquake.

She was in so much trouble.

"Are you okay now?" he asked.

Not really, she thought, but nodded anyway. "I'm not usually that emotional. But Emily was so excited.

She finally got her pony ride." Smiling she added, "More like the mother of all pony rides. Thank you, Cade."

"Don't mention it, ma'am."

Darn. He picked a heck of a time to turn on the charm. "Now that I know she's all right, I'd better get back to the house." She started to turn away.

"Not so fast," he said. "It's your turn."

Her heart fluttered. "Excuse me?"

"I'm going to teach you how to ride a horse."

"Why? I'm the camp cook. It's darn difficult to flip flapjacks on horseback."

"No one is asking you to ride and cook at the same time."

Her gaze narrowed on him. "I have the feeling that you're planning something that requires me to do both. Not necessarily at the same time or in that order."

"How do you do that?" he asked, his tone faintly amused.

"What?"

"Read my mind."

"Drat. I was hoping I was wrong."

He shook his head. "A boy becomes a man when he knows he can take care of himself."

"I can't argue with that logic, but I'm not sure I understand what that has to do with me." She didn't understand, but that didn't ease her bad feeling.

"I want to take the kids on an overnight campout and I need your help."

"Wouldn't an experienced ranch hand be of more use to you than a greenhorn English teacher?"

He shook his head. "This has nothing to do with the ranch except as part of the program my father started. That makes it one of your responsibilities. You know how to handle the kids. That's why I hired you."

She laughed. "Give me a break, Cade. For all the checking you did, I could have been an escaped mental patient. You hired me because my résumé was on the top of your stack. You had no choice."

"And you took the job because you had no choice. Now we're stuck with each other."

She folded her arms over her chest. "Okay."

"Okay," he answered.

Stubbornly, they stared at each other for several moments. Finally Cade said, "Since the day the kids got here you've been hounding me to let them see the ranch."

"Hound is such a strong word—"

"Are you afraid?"

"Afraid is such a strong word," she said, darting a nervous glance toward the barn.

"Come with me," he said, taking her hand.

"You can lead an English teacher to a horse," she grumbled. "But you can't make her ride."

"I won't let you get hurt."

If it was just about her apprehension of sitting on top of an animal big enough to toss her a long way to the ground and grind her into a bloody heap, she could have handled his nearness. But she was threatened by her attraction to him too.

She dug her tennis shoes into the dirt, and pulled her hand from his. "This isn't about you, Cade."

Calmly, he looked at her. "What is it about?"

"Me," she said, tapping her chest. "I've never been around animals. Patting Lady's neck was one thing. Sitting up high on a horse's back is a horse of a different color.''

''Never?''

She shook her head. ''Mom worked two jobs so she could feed my brother and me. No way was she going to waste hard-earned money on a pet.''

''What about your father?''

She shrugged, priding herself on her ability to tamp down the knot of resentment. ''He wasn't around.''

''I'm sorry—''

''Look,'' she said quickly, unwilling to talk about something best left alone. ''I didn't tell you that because I wanted your sympathy. It just explains my apprehension concerning animals. Big, big animals,'' she finished.

''Okay. I respect that. But I didn't figure you for the sort of person who doesn't practice what she preaches.''

''What's that supposed to mean?''

''You kept telling me I needed to get involved with the boys, even when I said I had nothing to offer. I was skittish, but I gave it a shot.''

''And?'' she prompted.

''It worked out okay.'' He shot her a challenging look. ''Are you willing to put your money where your mouth is? Will you try something you're afraid of?''

She met his gaze and the intensity in his blue eyes took her breath away. Was he talking about riding a horse? Or something even more dangerous?

Chapter Seven

Cade saw more than fear of horses in her eyes. She was afraid of him. Or rather being close to him. He hadn't missed the way she'd avoided touching. Now that he thought about it, she'd steered clear of him ever since he'd kissed her last night on the front porch. It didn't take a Ph.D. in psychology to figure out that she was scared of the attraction between them. Obviously she wanted to ignore anything personal, but he couldn't continue to deny that it existed.

Now wasn't a good time to deal with it. She'd encouraged him to make friends with the boys, and had slowly chipped away at his isolation. As much as he hated to admit it, he'd been wrong not to get involved first thing. Showing them how to ride had been fun, and rewarding in a way he hadn't expected. He wanted to return the favor and teach her that she didn't need to be nervous around horses.

Cade decided he wasn't going to let her get away

with her do-as-I-say-not-as-I-do attitude. It was P.J.'s turn to be the student.

The only answer he didn't have was how to convince her.

He looked at her self-consciously kicking the corral dirt with the grungy toe of her once-white sneaker. "I suppose I could take the boys without you," he said.

"Sure. Why not?" she agreed quickly. "Emily and I can stay here and hold down the fort while you guys do some serious male bonding on the trail."

He had a hard time suppressing a grin. She had just given him the angle he needed. "Yeah," he agreed. "There's only one problem that I can see."

Her forehead wrinkled in a puzzled frown. "Which part? The male bonding?"

"No. Emily."

"Why is she a problem? I don't understand."

"She won't take kindly to being left behind," he said.

P.J. frowned. "I hadn't thought about that."

"I'd be happy to take her—"

"Not without me," she said firmly. "And it's not that I don't trust you and the boys to keep her safe. I would worry like crazy."

"Then you have to learn something about horses before you get in the saddle—"

She started to shake her head. "She'll be okay with staying behind."

He laughed. "Get real, P.J. The Princess of Pout?"

"Sure. I can handle her."

"She wasn't too happy when the boys went to a movie without her. You saw how excited she was riding a horse. Do you honestly think she's going to accept being left out of an overnight trail ride?''

''I don't think—''

''Be honest. Do you really want to let your fear stand in the way of her experiencing the great outdoors? The countryside in all its glory? The miracle of Mother Nature?''

She put her hands on her hips. ''You're carrying that nature bit just a tad far, cowboy.''

''It's your call,'' he said, sticking his fingertips in his jeans pockets.

Cade watched her as she hesitated. She caught her full bottom lip between her teeth. He remembered the taste and texture of her mouth against his own and his breath caught for a moment. The attraction between them was definitely there, and getting stronger. At least on his part. It was more than just a testosterone surge around a pretty woman. The more he got to know her, the more he liked her. Somehow seeing this chink in her armor made him like her even more.

Before he could stop himself, he wondered ''what if?'' What if she cared about him enough to stay? Every time that thought crept into his mind, it was quickly followed by ''if only.'' If only he was the kind of man a woman like her could care for. Then there was Emily. Shaking his head, he reminded himself that he didn't have anything to offer either of them.

When the summer was over, he would have the ranch free and clear. Thanks in large part to P.J. But she and Emily would go back home. At least while she was here he could give her an appreciation of horseback riding.

''What do you say?'' he asked.

"I say riding horses is not in my job description."

"And?" he encouraged.

"Okay." She took a deep breath and slanted a narrow-eyed, apprehensive look at the barn. "I hope I don't live to regret this. Or worse, *not* live to regret it."

"I won't let you get hurt," he promised. Especially by me, he silently added.

He held out his hand, and to his surprise, she took it. He felt her trembling and squeezed her fingers reassuringly. She would only touch him because she was apprehensive. He knew that. But couldn't stop the brief flash of regret that it wasn't her desire to be close to him that motivated the contact.

They entered the empty barn. Correction, empty of people. The kids had finished their chores and gone to the house to clean up. He walked down the row of horses, quickly assessing the condition of each. Nodding with satisfaction, he couldn't find anything amiss in their work.

"The boys did a good job," he said to P.J.

"I'm glad you're not disappointed. I only hope I can uphold the high standard they've set."

"You'll do fine."

He looked at the horses, ticking off their characteristics in his mind. It was critical that he make the right choice for P.J. He didn't want to put her on one the boys had ridden. They'd already established a relationship which would be important when he took them trail riding. All of his stock were well trained. But P.J. needed an especially sweet-tempered animal. His gaze stopped at the second to last stall. Hunny. She'd earned her name for two reasons—the color of her coat and her disposition, smooth and sweet as honey. Perfect, he thought.

He gently but firmly tugged P.J. along with him to the stall, letting go only long enough to open the gate. Leading her inside he said, "This is Hunny."

"If you say so," she said, giving the animal a skeptical look.

"She's a perfect match for you, a real sweetheart," he continued. "You two are going to be great friends. Do you remember the night I showed Emily how to feed Lady?"

P.J. nodded as her eyes darkened with apprehension. "Is that absolutely necessary? I know they say the way to a man's heart is through his stomach—I'm sorry. I babble when I get nervous."

He decided not to read anything into the fact that she was his cook and well on her way down the trail to his heart. That wasn't a trail he would let her take. Concentrate on what you know, he told himself.

"But," she continued, "her mouth and teeth are so big. And—"

"We're going to start with something easy." Standing behind her, he took her hand and rested it on Hunny's neck. "Just touch her."

P.J. brought her arm down in a few tense movements. "Like this?" she asked.

Cade put his hands on her upper arms and caressed her. Just for moral support, he told himself. "Relax. I'm right here."

"I know," she said, her voice breathless. Whether from nerves, or him, or the closeness of their bodies, he wasn't sure. But he couldn't help hoping that her feelings for him had something to do with it.

"You need to get in close." He moved her gently

forward. The horse stood completely still, calmly waiting. "See how sweet-natured she is?"

"I'll take your word for it," P.J. answered.

"She wouldn't hurt a fly."

"What about one greenhorn English teacher from St. Bridget's?" she asked, dropping her arm.

Cade took her hand and placed it on the animal's neck again. "Just stroke her," he urged. "Long smooth movements. Pat her. Pretend she's a cat."

"Tough to do when she's not only looking down at me, but I couldn't begin to put her in my lap." In spite of her words, she did as he said.

With their bodies touching, Cade could read her state of mind. He knew the instant P.J. began to loosen up. She moved sideways and lengthened her touch from the neck to include the horse's back and flank.

"You're doing fine," he said. "You okay?" he asked.

"So far, so good. Now what?"

"Keep that up for a while. Believe it or not, she needs to learn that you're not going to hurt her."

"We're establishing a bond of mutual trust?"

He grinned. "Leave it to an English teacher who minored in psychology."

"Am I wrong?" she asked, glancing at him over her shoulder. Her eyes twinkled with humor.

"Nope." Without making a sound, he backed up a step.

"Where are you going?" she asked, instantly freezing up.

"Nowhere. Just giving you a little space to do that mutual bonding trust thing."

Just giving myself a little space to put a lid on my

lust, he thought. It wasn't easy with her curvy little backside pressed to his front. He had to forget about his own growing need and concentrate on helping her. Without distance, lust would win this round.

He moved around to Hunny's other side. From across the animal's neck, he studied P.J. Her delicate brows were drawn close with her effort to concentrate. Unconsciously, she ran her tongue across her full lips, making him groan inwardly. He couldn't decide which form of P.J. torture was worse—full body contact, or looking at her without being able to touch.

After a while, the intensity in her expression eased and she gave him a tentative smile. "She feels softer than I thought she would."

He nodded, and swallowed hard. He'd discovered the same thing about P.J., and she *looked* incredibly soft. She tasted even more incredible. He wanted to kiss her again, badly. He'd chosen wisely to put a horse between them. If he'd stayed cozied up to her the way they were, he would have pulled her into his arms and done what instinct was urging him to do. This teaching thing was turning into a bad idea.

"I think she likes me, Cade," P.J. said, the first note of excitement in her voice.

What's not to like? he wanted to shoot back. But instead he answered, "I think we're ready to go on to lesson two." From a corner of the stall, he pulled down the bridle.

"What is that?" she asked. "And where are the written instructions?"

He laughed. "Why do you insist on making this hard?"

"Defense mechanism," she answered. "If someone says it's easier than it looks, you know you're going to get flattened. If I can live with the bottom line, I know it'll be okay."

"I never figured you for a glass-is-half-empty kind of person."

"Really?"

He shrugged. "You hide that pessimistic streak behind your darned annoying cheerfulness."

"Don't you dare call me perky," she said, pointing her finger at him. Hunny shifted a little, and P.J. froze. "No sudden moves," she told the horse.

When the animal quickly settled, P.J. patted her neck again and said, "Good girl. I'm sorry I startled you. Hunny, you can call me anything you want." Then she shot him a triumphant look.

He held the bridle out so she could see the configuration. "These larger openings go over Hunny's ears. This metal part goes in her mouth."

"Whoa." P.J. looked apprehensive. "Do you think it's a good idea to stick a piece of metal in her mouth then expect her to like me?"

"Your goal is not to win friends and influence horses. It's getting the bit in her mouth without losing any fingertips."

"Good Lord," she breathed.

"Just watch." He held his hand out, fingers flat, with the bit in his palm and put it by Hunny's mouth. The well-trained animal immediately opened and took it, then he lifted the bridle straps over her ears. "See? Piece of cake."

"Easy for you to say. You've probably been doing that since you were knee-high to a grasshopper. Who taught you?"

"My father."

The words came out easily. The feelings didn't. For

so many years he'd remembered an unyielding, judgmental man. After leaving home, he hadn't wanted to think about that time. He'd put it all behind him, started fresh. Suppressed the memories. For some reason, they were starting to surface. For some reason, as a grown man, he was getting mixed impressions of Matt McKendrick.

The images came swiftly. His father firm, demanding perfection, as Cade learned to ride. Another mental picture haunted him—the rage and disappointment in his dad's eyes when he'd driven him home from the cop shop after letting him spend the night in jail. Everything changed as he'd grown up. He'd believed his father didn't understand anything. In Cade's mind, everything was black and white. Was there gray area that he'd refused to consider?

"I'll bet your father was a good teacher," she said gently.

How had she known he was thinking about his father? He looked at her, noting the softness in her brown eyes. They were like warm chocolate, sweet and comforting. He could easily get lost there. If he let himself.

"What makes you say that?" he asked.

"Because children learn what they live and you're a good teacher."

Her compliment touched a parched, dusty, lifeless part of his soul. He'd like to believe she meant that. More—he would like to believe it was true. But he'd spent a lot of years convinced that he couldn't do anything right. It had taken him a long time to leave behind that mixed-up teenager who'd vowed to make his way without anyone. Bull-riding on the rodeo circuit had taught him self-reliance. But he was still a loner.

Not sure how to respond to her words, he headed for solid ground. "The next step is the saddle blanket," he said. He pulled it from the stall fence, then handed it to her.

P.J. took the thick, quilted oblong blanket from him, not in the least offended when he ignored her praise. She'd watched him wrestle with it, and knew he was uncomfortable. It didn't surprise her that he didn't respond. She wished he could see himself as she did. A good man. The words were on the tip of her tongue, but just her saying them wasn't enough to convince him. She could only hope he would take the steps and come to the same conclusion she had.

In the meantime, she had to take some steps of her own. Like overcoming her apprehension of big animals. Like putting the blanket on the horse's back. Like controlling her physical and emotional response to a man clearly in conflict with his past. Until he put that into some kind of perspective, he was still wounded. The kind who could strike back and break her heart. No. Not hers. Because she wouldn't let herself care.

P.J. figured the best way to ignore her feelings was action. She spread the blanket over the horse's back, smoothing it out evenly.

Beside her, Cade brushed his palm over the material. "Always make sure that there are no wrinkles."

"Words to live by," she said, trying to still her body's reaction to his nearness. His warmth combined with the odors of aftershave and leather to wrap around her, burrowing inside her, pulling her to him, until she wanted to run in the opposite direction. But she stood her ground because she was a grown woman and that was no way to react.

"Wrinkles in the blanket could really hurt a horse. Once the saddle goes on, then a rider, if it's not absolutely smooth, she's going to be miserable." He gave her a serious look. "Have you ever worn shoes over a wrinkled sock? It works up a hellacious blister."

She nodded, forcing herself to concentrate on the words. "Been there, done that."

"The difference is that an animal will react instinctively to let you know something's wrong. If that happens, you might wind up with your backside in the dirt."

"And who could blame her?" P.J. said, stroking Hunny's nose.

He checked her arrangement of the blanket and she watched him. His hands were large, strong, competent. She marveled at his gentleness. The combination of tenderness and strength was amazingly sexy. Not to mention the fact that he was fiercely protective of his animals. Would he protect a woman he cared about as intensely?

She immediately pushed the thought away. That kind of information was on a need-to-know basis. She didn't need to know as it would never, ever impact her. She tried to think only about his words. Everything he said was simple, clear, and practical. He *was* a good teacher. Her heart swelled with admiration and something more intense.

"Any wrinkles?" she asked. There were more than she wanted to admit, but she was inquiring about the horse blanket.

He shook his head. "Time for the saddle." He

pointed to where it rested over the fence. "That's a western style. You should be able to lift it."

The straw beneath her sneakers rustled as she walked over to it and tested the weight. Finding it manageable, although bulky and clumsy, she carried it back to where Cade stood beside the horse.

She looked from him, to the animal, then to the leather seat and stirrups she held. "I can carry it, but I'm not sure I can put it on her. I'm afraid I'll hit her or scare her with it."

He nodded. Taking it out of her hands, he easily settled the contraption over Hunny's back.

"You make everything look simple," she said.

"It's easier if you have some height."

He certainly had that, she thought, admiring his tall, muscular body. Don't go there, she reminded herself. Keep this light.

"So you're calling me a little shaver?" she asked, struggling to force a grin.

"Nope," he answered. "I'd never call a lady names." He reached beneath the horse's belly and grabbed one wide leather strip with a buckle and the opposite strap, then hooked them together. "This is the cinch. If you don't buckle it, you're in for a real short ride. Then you need to check it and make sure it's snug, but comfortable for the horse. If it's not tight enough, the saddle will slip and you'll wind up on—"

"My backside in the dirt," she finished. Shaking her head, she said, "You're making this whole thing sound more appealing as you go along."

"Happy to be of service, ma'am."

When he grinned, she realized the inherent pitfall of keeping it light. That look—so rare, so dear—was deadly. If he kept it up too long, she would wind up with her backside in the dirt—emotionally speaking. She was quickly running out of weapons to fight him.

"Now what?" she asked.

"The moment of truth. What you've been waiting for. Time to put your fanny in the saddle."

"I'm doing the dance of joy." When he gave her a questioning look, she said, "Can't you tell how excited I am?"

One corner of his mouth lifted. "It's written all over your face." He held the stirrup steady. "Put your left foot in here, and one hand on the saddle horn to pull yourself up. Then swing your right leg over the horse's rump."

"I suppose there's no backing out?" Before he could respond, she said, "No guts, no glory."

Following his directions, she successfully mounted. The good news was she was very high up. The bad news was she was very high up. It was a bit scary, but exhilarating at the same time.

"You okay?" he asked.

"Fine as frog's hair," she said. "Don't ask me what that means."

"Didn't plan to. You're nervous and you're rambling again is all."

He was way too perceptive and knew her far too well. And she didn't like it a bit.

Ruefully, she looked down at the length of the stirrup and how high above it her foot was. "I don't claim to know much, but I've seen enough westerns to know that my foot is supposed to go in the stirrup. With nothing to brace myself, I could wind up on my backside in the dirt."

"I can fix that. All we have to do is adjust the

length.'' He did it, then took her ankle and placed her foot in the leather-encased triangle.

His strong fingers on her leg jump-started her heart. Not to mention the tingles the trail of his touch left behind.

"Okay," she said. "I've got the hang of this whole riding thing. What goes up must come down, and what could be easier than falling off a horse?"

She started to dismount.

"Hold it," he said. "We're not finished yet. What's your hurry?"

Chapter Eight

"I'm not in a hurry," she said a little too quickly.

Fib, he thought. She was well on her way to overcoming her aversion to horses, but he couldn't say the same about her fear of him. It couldn't be more obvious if she held out a crucifix and wore garlic around her neck. She couldn't wait to get away from him.

"There are a couple things you need to know to be trail safe."

"Like what?" She picked up the reins, one in each hand. "She walks. I hold on for dear life and hope for the best. What else do I need to know?"

"First of all, you hold both reins in your left hand." As he pulled them together and placed them in her palm, he didn't miss the shiver that rippled through her.

"Okay. But then how does she know which direction I want to go?"

"Move your hand to the right or left. She'll get the message. To stop, you pull back gently. To go, you nudge her with your heel, real easy. Or make a clicking noise. *Then* you hang on and hope for the best."

"Okay. Got it," she said and started to dismount again.

"Don't you want to try it in the safety of the corral?"

She shook her head. "It's getting late and there are four ravenous children up at the house. I've got to fix supper."

She awkwardly lifted herself out of the saddle and hung on tight as she set one foot in the hay. He couldn't resist putting his hands on her waist to steady her. When she freed her left foot from the stirrup and was firmly on the ground, she moved quickly away from him.

"I've got to get a meal on the table," she said again. "You must be hungry too."

You have no idea, he thought, letting his gaze rest on her mouth. But all he said was, "I could use a meal."

"It'll be ready in two shakes of a lamb's tail." She started through the stall gate, then turned to him. "Cade?"

"Yeah?" He set the saddle back on the fence and looked at her.

"Thanks for the lesson. Like I said, you're a very good teacher. I'm glad you made me try it. I'm not so afraid of horses anymore."

Then she was gone. He shook his head, wishing he was a better teacher. If he was, he would know how to help her over her fear of him. Then again, maybe she was right to keep her distance. They were friends. They liked and respected each other, although he wasn't quite sure what she saw in him. But what was between them should stay simple and uncomplicated. Taking the relationship any farther would make it that much harder to let her go.

He remembered his father's words about him not realizing what he had on the ranch. Matt McKendrick had called him a lot of things, not the least of which was ungrateful. He couldn't wish that P.J. had never come into his life. But how did he stop himself from wanting her to stay?

A week after her first riding lesson, P.J. was back in the saddle again. Cade was in the lead with Emily behind him. The little girl had protested that she wanted to ride with Steve. She was a big girl and would be eight on her next birthday. Cade had patiently explained that she could be a hundred and eight, but her horse was trained to follow his. P.J. knew he was only telling her that to placate her. He wanted her close to him so he could keep an eye on her. He'd put P.J. right after her daughter for the same reason—to be close to him.

After that the order was Todd, then Mark, with Steve bringing up the rear. She remembered the young man's flush of pride when Cade told him he'd taken to horses like a duck to water and he needed his cool-headed experience at the end of the line.

After the first hour and a half, she began to wish she had listened to Cade. He'd told her to accustom her body to the rigors of horseback riding before tackling the trail. She ached in places she hadn't known were there until today. After several hours on said trail, she almost wished her backside *was* in the dirt instead of the saddle that felt like a block of granite every time she bounced against it.

More than anything, she wished Em was taller. P.J. just wanted her big enough to block the view of Cade's broad shoulders. He was a pretty impressive sight and gave the expression "tall in the saddle" a whole new meaning. She sighed. Hiding behind her daughter made her wimp champion of the world.

Cade stopped his mount and the rest of the horses halted too. Herd instinct he'd called it.

"Listen up," he said.

The boys urged their animals closer to hear what he had to say. "Are we stopping here for the night?" Todd asked.

Cade nodded. "It's a good spot."

"Why?" Mark wanted to know.

"There's a stream over there," Cade answered pointing. "Can you guys swim?" All three boys nodded enthusiastically. He looked at Emily. "How about you, buckaroo?"

"'Course I can. I'm going to be eight pretty soon."

Not long after that they would be going home, P.J. remembered. The thought of returning to her life didn't excite her as much as she would have expected. Emily was thriving on the ranch. She hadn't once asked about the friends she'd left behind. And P.J. realized *she* hadn't missed home either. Her thoughts had been far too occupied by one handsome cowboy.

Cade surveyed the group of young people. "P.J. and I will keep an eye on you to make sure everyone is safe around the water. But everyone still has to look out for each other. The buddy system."

"I'll look out for Steve," Emily volunteered.

"Right back at ya', Em 'n' Em," he said with a grin.

P.J. marveled at the change in the teen. His hostility had disappeared since Cade had begun to take an interest in him. If she was meeting the boy for the first time, she would never guess that he was "at risk." She wondered what Matt McKendrick would think if he could see the way Cade was handling the program. Is this what he'd had in mind? The effects were beginning to show—in the kids and his son.

"Before anyone takes off," Cade continued, "see to your horses." He pointed to his right. "We'll let them graze in that meadow."

Steve easily dismounted. His fluid grace reminded her of Cade, and he didn't look sore at all. But he'd practiced every day as Cade had instructed. "Don't we have to tie up the horses?" he asked. "Won't they run away?"

We should be so lucky, P.J. wanted to say as her rear end throbbed.

But Cade shook his head. "They're tired. All they want is to be watered and fed."

One by one the kids dismounted, with Steve helping Emily to the ground. They led their horses to the spot Cade had pointed out and proceeded to take care of them as he'd instructed.

P.J. slid out of the saddle, her knees buckling slightly as she touched the ground. She held on until she knew the limbs that had turned into noodles would actually resume their function as legs.

Cade moved beside her. "I'll get that saddle for you. Why don't you sit down by the stream?"

"The last thing I need to do is sit," she said. "But

I would be more grateful than you can possibly know if you would see to my horse.''

"My pleasure, ma'am."

Quickly and efficiently he freed the animal from her trappings. Then Hunny happily trotted after his horse to join her friends contentedly grazing in the meadow. P.J. followed Cade to a lovely spot by the edge of the stream where they could keep an eye on the kids. The boys had slipped off their jeans and shirts to the swimming attire they'd put on underneath. Em had done the same and was now happily splashing in the water.

P.J. leaned her back against a tree, unwilling to plant her rear end on anything as hard as the fallen tree stump that Cade indicated. He stood beside her, his arms folded over his chest, brown hat pulled low on his forehead, shielding his eyes from the late afternoon sun.

Sighing deeply, she listened to the kids' shrieks of laughter. The beauty of the trees and blue sky above enveloped her. She was content.

"I wish I could stay here forever," she said dreamily.

"Okay."

His deep voice startled her. She had almost forgotten he was there. *Almost.* Who was she kidding? It was impossible to stand this close to a man like Cade McKendrick and forget his presence. He exuded sensuality and power. He made her think about what could be if she ever learned to trust. That thought nearly distracted her from what he'd said.

"Okay?" she repeated. "What does that mean?"

He glanced at her, eyes hidden by the shadow of

his hat. "Seems simple enough for a wordmeister like you to understand."

"It's not the word I'm questioning." Just everything it could possibly mean, she thought. "As much as I might like to, I can't stay here forever."

"Why not?"

"Two reasons, and that's right off the top of my head. My house and my job." She didn't mention the third reason because it was all about him.

"That's all?" he asked.

There was that darn ability of his to pay attention to her and figure out what she was thinking. Of course there was something else. Her attraction to him. That scared the stuffing out of her. She was already teetering on the brink of something serious. If she stayed past the summer... That didn't bear thinking about.

"I have a career nine months of the year. And a daughter to support. I can't turn my back on my responsibilities and run away."

"Okay."

She glanced at him. He'd pushed his hat to the back of his head but she still couldn't tell what he was thinking. What did okay mean? Was he anxious for her to go? Or did he want her to stick around?

Her heart caught and so did her breath. For just an instant, she wished that he'd begged her to forget her other life and stay with him. She wished he would declare his intention to take care of her. More than anything she wished she could let herself believe it if he did say the words.

But she couldn't.

Men didn't keep their promises. They didn't stay. And they didn't take care of their families. She would be a fool to turn her back on the life she'd made for herself and Em, and believe in a cowboy's promise. She was worse than a fool for giving the notion even this much thought.

"Okay," she echoed.

One small word. Two syllables, that effectively closed the door on the dangerous subject of expectations. Long ago she'd decided it would be best not to have any hopes. It was too hard to watch them drop-kicked into oblivion.

If only she could find the right word, or combination of syllables, to shut down her feelings.

Cade lay on his back near the dying campfire. With his bedroll beneath him, he tucked his hands under his head and looked up at the stars. The boys were asleep on the other side of the fire. P.J., with Emily beside her, slept next to him. He could hear the child's even breathing. But her mother was tossing and turning restlessly.

He wondered if she was thinking about him, or whether sore muscles from the ride kept her awake. Thoughts of one pretty English teacher had been interrupting his rest ever since she'd showed up for the job. He tried to picture his life after she went back to hers. Instantly he shut down the bleak mental image.

He heard P.J. sit up and glanced in her direction. In the moonlight, he saw her stretch, then groan softly. Carefully she leaned to the side lifting one hip, then the other, repeating the movement. Finally she slipped on her sneakers, stood and tiptoed in the direction of the stream.

Every instinct he had urged him to follow her. Every defense mechanism in his body said he would be a fool to go. His father's words popped into his head. *Don't run away from your problems. They go where you go.*

"I'm not sleeping anyhow," he mumbled softly. He sat up and leaned on his elbows, glancing around quickly. All the kids were still sleeping soundly, tuckered out from the day's activity.

He sat up, slipped on his boots, and followed P.J. to the spot where they'd talked earlier.

"P.J.?" he called softly so as not to startle her.

"Cade?" she whispered back as he came through the trees.

He stopped and looked down at her. "Did I scare you?"

"A little." Her palm was on her chest. "My heart is going a mile a minute."

"Sorry. I didn't want to shout and wake the kids." He tucked his fingertips in his jeans. The nearly full moon made it easy to study her. She looked tired. "You can't sleep?"

She nodded. "I've never camped out before. Sleeping on the ground is tough to get used to."

"Is that the only reason?"

"My muscles are sore too. Satisfied?" she asked.

"I'd never say I told you so to a lady. The code of the West and all."

"Yeah. I'd like to take that code, along with my saddle and drop it like a stone in that stream over there."

"What you have is nothing more serious than greenhornitis."

She grinned up at him. "Don't be charming. I'm not in the mood for it. And I hate it when you do that."

He smiled back and ignored her. "It's not fatal," he continued.

"Greenhornitis or your charm?" she asked.

"Take your pick."

"Then I choose greenhornitis. Because from where I'm standing, it feels fatal," she said stretching.

"I can help."

She froze. "I don't want to play doctor with you."

"What I have in mind is nothing more than the treatment of the trail."

"And that would be?"

"Rubbing where it hurts." He looked down at her. Big mistake, he thought.

In the moonlight, her eyes looked huge. Strands of brown hair framed her face, free and wild, as if she'd just come from a man's bed. The thought sent his blood racing through his veins, rushing south to the male part of him that instantly reached out to her femininity. He saw the pulse-point in her neck throbbing frantically and knew she felt the same things he did. But instead of answering, she just stared up at him, eyes wide, her lower lip caught between her teeth.

He moved behind her and put his hands on her shoulders. "So where does it hurt?" When she shivered, he asked, "Are you cold?"

"N-no."

The evening was pleasant and cool, far from cold. He knew he was right about her response to him. "Tell me where it hurts."

"Places you can't see," she whispered.

"What?" he asked.

She cleared her throat. "I said in places that you

need to leave be. Suffice it to say my shoulders and back are killing me."

He grinned as he began kneading the tight muscles. "I bet that's not all."

She groaned and sighed at the same time. "Heaven," she breathed.

No, but it could be, he thought. Just be a friend, he warned himself. But with her this close, and smelling like flowers in a meadow, silver moonlight surrounding them, her delicate flesh beneath his hands. He could caution himself from now till next year and it wouldn't help.

He turned her until she faced him, then folded her into his arms. She made a token move to pull away, but he tightened his hold.

"What are you afraid of?" he asked.

"Nothing," she answered, a little too quickly, a bit too breathlessly.

"Hogwash," he said, trying to tamp down his annoyance. "You've been giving me a wide berth ever since that night I kissed you on the front porch."

"So?"

Though he could feel her need to move away, he didn't want to let go. He continued to hold her. "Tell me why."

She shrugged, the movement shooting for indifference, but ending up a shiver. "I'm not a tease. I don't believe in starting something I can't finish."

"What if I want to start it?"

"I'm sorry. I don't."

"Another fib, Miss Goody Two-Shoes. And I can prove it." He lowered his mouth to hers.

For a heartbeat she resisted. Then her mouth softened and she kissed him back. Her arms circled his waist and her hands slid up his back. He pressed her closer to his length, enjoying the feel of her breasts against him. A warning sounded in his head, but he ignored it.

He put one arm behind her knees and the other across her back, lifting her. She gasped, startled, as he carried her closer to the gurgling stream and sat down on the fallen log, then settled her in his lap.

He rested his forearm on her thighs and slanted his lips across hers. She tasted of softness and heat. The promise of passion was there too. His heart pounded and instinct took over. He could no more stop himself than he could halt a runaway locomotive by standing on the tracks.

Lifting his hand, he cupped her breast in his palm, his breath catching at the sweetness of the perfection he held. He felt her hesitation, then her surrender to the sensation. When she opened her mouth, he slipped his tongue inside, caressing the moist, welcoming warmth. He placed small, nibbling kisses on her nose and mouth, then moved to her neck and a delicate spot beneath her ear that earned him a serious shiver.

She put a hand on his shoulder and pushed gently. "This is a bad idea," she said breathlessly.

"Why? What are you afraid of?" he asked, his own voice husky with frustrated desire.

He couldn't shake the feeling that her reluctance was much more than a broken marriage making her skittish. She'd already told him her ex-husband let her and Em down. But he sensed there was something more holding her back.

"I'm not afraid," she answered defensively.

"Then it's me. Brown-hat syndrome."

P.J. kicked herself for making him feel responsible.

Her inability to commit had nothing to do with him and she hated that he immediately blamed himself.

"No." She rested her small hand on his cheek. "You're a good man. I like you a lot."

"Then what's wrong?"

She didn't see any point in talking about it. Putting feelings into words wasn't helpful. "I meant what I said about not starting something I can't finish. We come from two different worlds. You can't leave yours and I have to go back to mine. When I do, I want to know that I have your friendship."

Cade took a deep breath and released it. "I hate it when you're practical."

"Yeah, me too." She couldn't stop herself from spreading her fingers through the hair falling over his forehead. Brushing it back, she sighed. "But that's who I am. P.J. the Practical."

He stood up and set her on her feet. "I'm sorry."

"No need—"

She saved her breath. He was already disappearing into the darkness.

Alone, she couldn't decide if she was disturbed because he'd made a move, or that he'd given up so easily. Or both. She couldn't shake the feeling that he'd expected her rejection. That he was comfortable with it. She felt awful, for him and herself.

But she'd done the right thing. He needed a woman who could be his equal, his match—his partner. Not one like her, who couldn't trust any man to stick around.

Sometimes she hated being right.

Chapter Nine

"**I** already told you, Em. I'm shopping for your birthday. I can't take you with me."

"But I don't want to stay here by myself." Emily plopped herself at the kitchen table, folded her arms and rested her chin on them.

"You're not by yourself." P.J. pulled the keys from her purse. "Steve and the guys are here. And Cade," she added softly.

Even as she said the encouraging words, P.J. knew they were a lie.

"Uh-uh," the little girl said, confirming the falsehood. "I can't find Steve. Mark and Todd are doing chores and they won't let me help, because Mr. Cade isn't here to watch me."

Unfortunately, Em didn't miss much. Several weeks had passed since they'd returned from the campout, and Cade had reverted to the same standoffish man who had tried to ignore them all at the beginning of the summer.

P.J. felt responsible. Because in her heart, she knew it had something to do with her shutdown by the stream. After that night, she could count on two hands the total words he'd said. But when she read between the lines, she came up with some astonishing questions every time. Did he want her to stay? If so— why?

In his arms by that same, infamous stream, she had wished he could hold her forever. Even now, the memory produced a shiver of excitement—just as it had the countless times she'd thought about it since. Every single time, the pleasure was effectively replaced by an ache of loneliness. And she had no one to blame but herself. She had pushed him away.

P.J. the Practical. P.J. the Idiot.

She told herself it was for the best. With all her heart she tried to believe that. But there were definitely strong feelings between them. On both sides. And he didn't have a clue why she couldn't act on them. If she explained, he might understand and maybe forgive.

"How come we don't see Mr. Cade anymore?" Emily asked.

P.J. shot a glance to her daughter. So she *had* felt it. Time for evasive action, she thought. "Of course we see him."

Still resting her chin on her arms, Emily turned her head to the side and looked at her. The expression on the child's small face oozed disgust, disappointment, but most of all hurt. It said more clearly than words that she couldn't be fooled or distracted by any fast talk. It was also the reason P.J. had put on the brakes for anything between herself and Cade. She would never let Em be disillusioned like she had been.

"Mo-om, I'm not a little kid. He used to eat dinner with us. And he showed me and the boys horse stuff and he let me help with chores and watched me around Lady." Angrily, she sat up and brushed stray hairs away from her face. "Ever since the campout he doesn't come home till after we're in bed. And he's always working far away from the ranch. I never get to do anything with Lady anymore."

"I don't know what to tell you, kidlet." There's nothing I can say that you would understand, she silently amended. Although it gave her no satisfaction, she'd been right about Cade. When he was wounded, he hurt back. Not overtly, but by retreating.

Emily stood up and jammed her hands in her jeans pockets. "No way now I'll get a horse for my birthday," she mumbled. "Or the other thing I want."

"What other thing?" She pulled the list from her pocket and the words at the bottom tugged at her heart. *A horse and a dad.*

P.J. took her daughter's hand and tugged her back to the table. She sat on a chair and pulled Em close, putting her arms around the child. "Sweetie, I told you not to get your hopes up for a dad. If I could go to the store and buy one, bring him home and put a ribbon around his neck, you would get one for your birthday."

Emily giggled slightly. It was just this side of pitiful, but it was enough to convince P.J. that she was getting through.

"Mr. Cade would look funny wearing a ribbon," she said.

If it would dim the power of his masculinity a couple of watts, P.J. thought, she would tie one on him herself. But she knew it wouldn't. If anything, she could picture the sheepish grin he would sport along with the bow. The mental image was enough to kick her heart rate up and make her grateful she was sitting down.

P.J. rested her cheek against her daughter's. "Em, I promise you'll have a wonderful birthday."

She put the list back in her pocket. Before she could clear the lump from her throat and decide what else to say, the kitchen door banged open. Mark stood there, half-carrying Steve. The latter was mumbling incoherently.

P.J. jumped up and rushed over to them, automatically looking for blood. "What's wrong?" she asked, not finding any.

"He's sick," Mark answered evasively.

Some part of her mind registered the fact that this was the first time she'd seen Mark without his baseball hat. Then she went into professional mode and took Steve's other arm, pulling it over her shoulders as she grabbed him around the waist. The smell of alcohol was strong.

She looked at Emily. "Go tell one of the ranch hands to find Cade."

The little girl nodded, a frightened look in her eyes. P.J. was relieved that she didn't argue to stay with Steve. Sooner or later her daughter had to grow up. But she would rather it was later.

Losing a hero was a painfully hard lesson.

It was late afternoon by the time Cade got the message about Steve, and returned to the house. The teenager had passed out cold after Mark and P.J. had put him on his bed. She had sent all the kids outside and one of the hands was keeping them busy. Cade was glad she'd sent for him. She wasn't physically strong enough to handle the kid by herself. Taking care of a drunken teenager was definitely not in her job description.

"Cade, don't make any rash decisions about sending him away."

Until she said the words, he hadn't realized he'd been considering it. "Next to that bottle, there were matches and cigarettes, P.J." He stared hard at her, letting the magnitude of the situation sink in. "The barn could have gone up like a matchstick. The hay, the horses—"

"I know this is serious," she said, dragging a hand through her already wild hair. "That just shows how much he needs guidance."

She expected him to guide Steve. If he didn't know better, he'd swear she took a header off a horse and it wasn't her backside that hit first. He couldn't even guide himself, let alone this troubled kid.

"I've said from the beginning that he's a loose cannon," he added.

"Yes, you have. But he's been a model teenager since you let him work with the horses. He's developed a sense of responsibility. All we need to do is figure out what made him slip up."

With her big brown eyes full of worry, she hardly looked more than a kid herself. He wanted to wrap his arms around her and tell her it would be fine. Or not to care so much. It hurt to care. But he knew she didn't want anything from him. Not his support or anything else. No matter how much he liked her, he couldn't change that.

Would he change it if he could? Would he give to her and take in return? The answer was yes. Because he was selfish. He would consume her sweetness and savor the comfort of just being around her. And he would do it even though he knew he had nothing but himself to offer her in return.

"Let's get him cleaned up," he said. "We can play psychiatrist later." Cade didn't need a shrink; he was the reason Steve had slipped up.

"Okay, no psychobabble," she said, looking at him from the other side of the bed. "Can you help me take his shirt off?"

He nodded. P.J. leaned over and unhooked the buttons. "I'll pull his arm out of the sleeve, then you roll him over and we'll slip it off."

"Okay."

They worked together and got the soiled shirt out from under him. Wrinkling her nose, she said, "I'll take this down to the washing machine."

He nodded and watched her walk out of the room, admiring her shapely backside and the feminine sway of her hips. For the last week and a half, he'd tried almost everything to forget the feel of her on his lap, in his arms, her body pressed to his, the sensation of her lips against his own. He'd tried not seeing her. Riding out to work on fences before sunup and coming back after dinner. He saw as little of her and the kids as he could. Nothing he'd done had erased the memory or blurred the intensity of his feelings.

In a few minutes, she returned with a basin of soapy water and a washcloth. She tenderly wiped Steve's face and hands, then smoothed the matted hair from his forehead. He mumbled incoherently, then began to snore.

"Cade?" She met his gaze. "Maybe we should get him to drink coffee."

He shook his head. "Then we'll have a wide-awake drunk on our hands. It's best if we let him sleep it off."

"Then help me roll him onto his side," she said.

"Why?"

"If he gets sick again, it could be dangerous if he's on his back."

"You're right."

She shrugged. "Once a mom—"

He smiled at her, wishing he could dislike her. That would make this whole thing easier. Liquor was the only thing he *hadn't* tried to get her out of his mind. What he'd found in the last week was that he could avoid them, but they were with him everywhere he went. Especially P.J.

"I'm going to get back to work," he said.

She glanced from him to the snoring teen. "Is it all right to leave him like this? Should I stay?"

"You really care about him, don't you?"

She nodded. "I like kids in general. But there's something especially endearing about Steve. He's so needy. And he tries to hide it, but he's thriving with just a little attention."

"You love him."

"Yeah," she said simply.

"Yeah," he echoed softly.

"Do you think he'll be okay—" A loud snore interrupted her.

Cade smiled. "The ceiling might need a little plaster repair. But other than a nasty hangover, he won't be the worse for wear."

"Then I guess I'll go back downstairs."

Before she left, she stopped briefly in the doorway to look at the teenager. Her maternal instincts were

on high alert. Then her warm, brown-eyed gaze rested
on him and his pulse quickened. The maternal look
was gone, replaced by an expression that was just for
him. He didn't think she even knew it was there.

That does it, he thought. He was going to find out
what was holding her back.

"See you at dinner?" she asked.

"Count on it," he said.

Tired and emotionally drained from the day's crisis, P.J. finished cleaning up the kitchen after a very
late dinner. Steve, sobered up and nursing the mother
of all hangovers, had joined them. Looking mega-
green around the gills, he hadn't downed much food,
but Cade had made sure he got fluids of the nonal-
coholic variety into him. She still didn't know if Cade
planned to cut short Steve's time in the program because of what he'd done.

The drinking was bad enough. She was glad the
other two boys hadn't joined him. They all looked up
to Steve and she knew how powerful peer pressure
could be. What worried her more was the matches. In
the hands of someone not in full control of his fac-
ulties, they could have been deadly.

She had seen that in Cade's eyes when he'd mentioned it to her earlier. She had expected him to take
Steve aside after dinner and break the bad news that
he had to go. But when they'd finished eating, all the
kids, including Emily, had accepted his invitation to
go outside. She hadn't seen hide nor hair of anyone
since.

It was dark now. Getting close to Emily's bedtime.
Just then the kidlet in question burst in the back door.

"Hey, you. What's going on?" she asked. "I was

just about to send the posse to look for you. It's bath time.''

''Not yet, Mommy. Please. We're having a camp-fire, like we did on the campout. Only it's in the bar-becue pit behind the house on account of we don't want to set anything on fire that we shouldn't.''

P.J. smiled. ''Did Cade tell you guys it was all right?''

Emily's little body nearly vibrated with excitement. ''He started it, Mom. I just came in for a sweatshirt. We're talkin'.''

P.J. hid her surprise. What had happened to the tall, dark, handsome, monosyllabic man who had found the far reaches of the wide-open spaces so fascinating recently? The answer frightened her. She would bet everything she owned that the same nice man who had coaxed her past her fear of horses was holding court around that campfire. *That* was the one who could destroy her safe, secure, carefully constructed life.

Don't overreact, she cautioned herself. There was only a short time left until she and Em headed for the familiar hills of home. Despite the ups and downs of the ranch she still didn't yearn for the sanctuary of her job at St. Bridget's or her quiet, cowboy-free life.

''It's getting late, Em. If you don't get enough sleep—''

''Please, Mom. Not yet.'' She put her hands to-gether, in a prayerful gesture. ''If you let me stay up a little longer, I'll even take a nap tomorrow.''

A nap? There must be something exciting going on around that campfire. ''Let me think about it.''

Her daughter nodded, then raced upstairs. Puzzled, P.J. stared into the space the child had just vacated.

Emily never missed an opportunity to let everyone within shouting distance know that she was a big girl. If she was willing to barter a nap for a bedtime reprieve, she must really want to be with Cade.

P.J. had learned one hard and fast rule in her experience as a teacher. Kids didn't suffer fakes easily. They could spot insincerity a mile away and avoided it like the plague. That meant Cade really wanted to hang out with them.

"I'm in really big trouble. Again," she added softly.

Emily reappeared. "Can I stay up, Mommy? Please? Pretty please with sugar on it?"

How could she say no? Besides, what could it hurt? "Okay."

"Thank you. I promise I'll be good tomorrow." She raced to the door, then stopped. "Come with me, Mom."

No way, P.J. thought. But she said, "I have work to do. Maybe I can make it before you guys are finished."

"Mo-om, you can do that stuff later—"

"Don't argue, Em." The wounded look in her daughter's eyes told her that her voice was sharper than she'd intended. "I'm sorry, kiddo. I didn't mean to be cross. But don't forget this is my job. We're not here on vacation."

Emily ran over to where she stood by the sink. She wrapped her arms around P.J.'s waist. "I'm sorry too, Mom. But please try and come."

"I will, sweetie."

The door closed and P.J. turned back to the empty sink she had just scoured. It reminded her of her life: spotless, shiny, clean—empty, lonely, cold.

She went to the back window and looked out. In the distance she spotted the flicker and glow of the fire. Maybe they'd like some marshmallows to roast. She went to the pantry and pulled out an unopened bag left over from the campout.

"No."

Tossing it back in the pantry, she shook her head and turned away from the temptation she could see through the window. Folding her arms over her chest she leaned against the counter and surveyed the spotless kitchen. Her work here was done.

"Funny how fibs have a way of coming back to bite you in the rear," she said to herself. "Work is *not* what's keeping you from that campfire. If only he looked like Gabby Hayes and acted like Black Bart."

Sighing, she tried to think of something to keep her occupied and out of harm's way with Cade.

She could search and destroy dust bunnies underneath the refrigerator. Scrape the fabric-softener buildup off the dispenser in the washer. Go upstairs and organize her sock drawer.

Go outside with Cade and the kids.

"Who are you trying to kid, Penelope Jane. That's where you really want to be."

When she and Emily were safely back home, would this feeling of yearning to be with him go away? Was it only because she could that she wanted to see him? Out of sight, out of mind? Was that the answer? It was definitely the solution. But not possible for a little while yet.

In the meantime, what could it hurt to go out and join them? He had told her early on that he wasn't interested in being a husband or a father. She had nothing to fear but herself.

"I'll throw caution to the wind," she said. "And pick up the pieces later."

If she was lucky, her heart would stay whole and there wouldn't be any pieces to pick up.

She went upstairs and grabbed a sweatshirt to throw around her shoulders. August evenings could get cool. Unless Cade had his arms around her.

"Stop that," she said out loud. "Just be sociable. Nothing more. And quit talking to yourself."

She went out the kitchen door and walked the short distance to the group around the fire. Before she'd come here, she'd thought ranch life was outhouses, cooking over an open fire, heating cans of beans, and lots of dirt. She'd found something very different. There was roughing it and there was comfortable ranch living. Cade's patio definitely fell into the latter category. The cement slab was trimmed in brick and sported the large fire pit as well as a built-in brick barbecue.

The fire had been started with wood and every time it crackled, sparks sprayed upward, trailing off into the black night. Cade and the kids were in padded redwood chairs around the circle. Well, not all the kids. Emily sat on his lap, with her head cradled on his shoulder. P.J. smiled at the tender picture. If they were a painting in need of a title, she would call them "Rugged cowboy holding sleepy little girl." The sight squeezed her heart and brought a lump to her throat.

"Evening, guys," she said.

"Mommy, you came." The sleepiness in Emily's voice made it husky.

"I did, sweet pea."

"Hey, Peej," Mark said.

"Hi." Todd, loose-limbed and relaxed, half sat, half reclined. He didn't move.

"P.J." Steve's voice was deep and reserved.

She guessed he was still feeling the effects of his hangover, not to mention the embarrassment of his misdeed.

"What's going on?" she asked.

She glanced around the circle. One by one she looked into their faces. Her gaze came to rest on Cade and she saw there a mirror image of the teenagers. Pain, anger, disillusionment were in his eyes. And weariness.

He looked tired. Deep lines carved his face on either side of his nose and mouth. As hard as she tried to ignore it, tenderness swelled in her heart. For him.

Cade looked down at Emily, asleep now. "We're just hanging out," he said.

"That's nice." P.J. held up the bag of marshmallows she'd retrieved from the pantry. "Anyone want to roast these?" she asked.

Steve groaned and even in the firelight she could see that he was pale. "I'll pass."

"Anyone else?" she said to Todd and Mark.

The former stifled a yawn and shook his head. "I'm about ready to hit the sack. We have to get up early tomorrow."

Mark nodded. "You can't get up at the crack of dawn and party on. I'm going to bed," he said, standing.

The other two teens did the same. They said their good nights and started to walk away.

"Steve?" she said.

He turned back. "Yeah?"

"Would you mind carrying Emily to the house? Just put her in bed. I'll tuck her in shortly."

"Sure thing," he said, taking the slumbering child from Cade.

When they were gone, he looked at her. "Now that we're alone, is there something you wanted to say?"

Chapter Ten

It continued to surprise her how well he could read her feelings. Had a man *ever* taken the time to notice what was going on with her? Cade had zeroed right in on her. There was definitely something she wanted to say. And she would. In her own good time.

"Do you mind if I sit down?"

Looking relaxed, he leaned back in the chair with his legs stretched out and boots crossed at the ankle. "Be my guest," he said.

He held out his hand, indicating the place beside him that Steve had just vacated.

It wasn't a good idea to be that close to him. She wanted to distance herself and put the fire between them because, she thought wryly, there was enough heat between her and Cade to warm the Alaskan tundra for the winter. But, P. J. Kirkland was no coward. She sat next to him and folded her arms over her chest.

"Don't keep me in suspense," she said. "Have

you made a decision about Steve? There's only a couple weeks left of summer anyway. I think it would help him so much to see that he can't push people away that easily. You've already—''

"He stays." He looked at her.

She blinked once, then let out a long breath. "I'm glad. That's such a relief."

"It's the right thing." He stared into the wavering flames. "Some of the blame for what he did is mine."

"How do you figure that?"

As she waited for him to answer, she breathed deeply, taking in the scent of wood smoke, mixed with the essence that was unmistakably Cade's. She closed her eyes for a moment and let the fragrance surround her. Oddly, she felt safe. Then her body began to tingle expectantly. She reminded herself that a dash of security mixed with a dollop of desire was a formula for a broken heart.

But all the warnings in the world didn't help when he sat there looking as sexy as sin. She wished he would say something, anything to take her mind off the deliciously masculine pose he presented.

"Why are you to blame, Cade?" she prompted.

"We were talking before you came out here." He paused a moment. "There's something about a campfire that makes you want to sit around it and talk. Tonight we discussed the pros and cons of drinking too much. Among other things."

"I think they needed that. It's good for them." Not to mention you, she wanted to say. "And?" she prompted again.

"I always thought I had it rough growing up. But those kids have me beat, P.J." There was anger, frustration and sympathy in his voice. "Did you know

Steve ran away from home after his mother's boy-friend knocked him around?''

"He never told me that. How could a mother put her own needs above the welfare of her child?'' she asked, furious at the thought. "A parent's job is to protect and defend her young."

"Then there's an epidemic of neglect. Todd's be-ing raised by his grandmother. Mark never even met his dad." He sighed, but it was an angry sound.

"Why do you feel responsible for what Steve did?''

"I treated him just like everyone else."

"You never hit him," she defended.

"Not physically. But he picked up on my feelings and figured out he wasn't wanted."

"That was just in the beginning. Cut yourself some slack. You came around and worked with the kids."

"You get the credit for that, P.J." He glanced side-ways at her. "It was because of you that I started to pay attention to him and the others."

"I still don't see why this makes you responsible for what he did."

"I shut him out again. He was trying to get my attention."

"It's called acting out," she said smiling. "And as attention-getters go, it was right up there at the top of the list."

"Yeah. The point is, he shouldn't have had to do that. Not now, and not when he arrived." He stared into the fire. "I'm not proud of the way I behaved in the last week."

"Typical passive/aggressive behavior."

"What does that mean?''

"That you were actively trying to ignore the kids."

"That diagnosis is not quite on the mark, Doctor. They got caught in the fallout." He met her gaze. "But mostly I was trying to forget about you."

Her heart began to flutter wildly. "Me?" she asked, the one syllable a squeak because she was barely able to make a sound.

"Just now, when you asked why I felt responsible, it took me a while to decide how much I should say."

"You say more in a couple words than most people can in a monologue."

"Is that a compliment?"

"Yes."

"Thanks. Because I have more to say. But I also have a sneaking suspicion you're not going to like it."

She wanted to run far, run fast. But again she reminded herself that she was not a coward. She especially couldn't head for the hills after his confession about his own retreat.

"Try me," she said, more confidently than she felt.

"Okay. I think you know that I'd like you to stay on when the summer program is over."

Her stomach dropped. She waited several moments for him to say more. At first she wasn't sure what she was expecting. Then she realized—she wanted him to give her a reason to stay. To tell her that he cared. Disappointment was heavy on her heart when he didn't.

She looked at her hands, intertwined in her lap. "I'd hoped I was wrong."

"You weren't." He leaned forward and rested his forearms on his knees as he stared into the fire. "I guess it was stupid to think that a woman like you would see anything in a guy like me."

"That's where you're wrong, cowboy." She put her hand on his arm and left it there when he tensed. No matter what the damage to herself, she had to touch him. Somehow, she had to communicate to him what she'd known all along—he was a fine, decent man. "I'm going to tell you this one more time. You're a hero, Cade."

He made a scoffing noise, then stared at her as if she'd lost her marbles. "Yeah. Right." His voice dripped sarcasm. "That's why Steve had to do what he did just to get me to notice him."

"You're a *good* man. Not perfect." She shifted to the edge of her chair and wrapped both hands around his upper arm. She felt the impressive muscle there, evidence of his physical power. But she knew he possessed strength of character too. She willed him to hear, understand, and take her words to heart. "Do you think you're exempt from mistakes?"

"I'm the adult. I should know better."

"How do you figure? You had a flawless childhood? If you're such a loser, tell me why your father went to such lengths to make sure you implemented his program."

"It's his way of punishing me from the grave."

"He's trying to tell you something, but it's not about punishment."

"I don't know what else it could be."

She shook his arm then stood up and glared at him. "For Pete's sake, when are you going to let that go? The reason he trusted you is as plain as the well-formed, patrician nose on your face."

"Does patrician mean big honker? Because I can't see what you're driving at."

For a bright man, he could be awfully dense. She

smiled in spite of her annoyance. Then her grin faded. The warmth of the fire was at her back; the heat of the man was in front of her. She'd sure as shootin' set up camp between a rock and a hard place. *And* she was out of the frying pan into the fire. Or any number of clichés she could think of that meant she was in hot water up to her eyebrows. With an effort, she pulled in her wayward thoughts and forced herself to focus.

"I'm driving at the fact that your father loved you, Cade."

"Then why did he dangle the ranch in front of me to get me to do what he wanted? Why not just ask?"

"Would you have done it?" He hesitated and she said, "That's why. He wasn't sure of you any more than you were of him. Your relationship was strained. You hadn't seen each other since you were a hard-headed teenager. You left home an angry kid and didn't come back until there was no time to repair the relationship as an adult. Emotionally, you hadn't matured past that rebellious eighteen-year-old. Why would he believe you cared enough about him to fulfill his dying wish? He didn't have enough time to establish a bond. He had to do something and that's what he came up with."

"Some solution," he said sarcastically.

"It worked, didn't it? I think he knew you better than you want to admit. He didn't trust your love for him, but he knew how much you cared about the ranch. And now that you're almost finished with the program, tell me you think it's a bad thing."

"I could lie."

She shook her head. "Not on a bet, cowboy."

His hands dangled between his knees. "I wish I

could say the whole summer was a complete waste of time." He shook his head in wonder. "The kids seemed to enjoy it. I guess they learned a thing or two."

"It's more than that. You taught them. It's been amazing watching the transformation. They're like neglected plants. With just a little water and fertilizer, they're blossoming."

"I've noticed that too." He looked up at her and she read irony in his expression. "And something I didn't count on. The truth is, I've learned a lot about myself."

"I think your father set this program in motion because he felt he failed you."

The look he gave her was pure disbelief. "Matt McKendrick never failed at anything."

"Exactly my point. You turned out pretty okay. So are you ready to admit that he might be responsible for starting a good thing? For the kids, and for you?"

"I still don't think I have anything to offer them," he said.

"What you give them doesn't come gift-wrapped with a big red bow. It's subtle. Solid. Honest. It's just being there for them."

He shot her a quizzical look. "You've said that before. Are *you* ready yet to tell me who wasn't there for you?"

"No." She turned away from him and folded her arms over her chest as she stared into the fire. Before she'd left the sanctuary of the kitchen, she had decided he should understand where she was coming from. Now that she had an opening, saying the words was much harder than she'd thought. "I would rather forget about it—"

"You can't forget. It's part of who you are. That's what I learned today. I tried to run. In fact I've been running for a long time. But there's nowhere to hide. All the bad stuff comes with you everywhere you go."

"You didn't let me finish," she said. "I don't *want* to talk about it, but it's about time you know why I have to go home."

Cade winced at her use of the word "home." He'd hoped she was beginning to think of the ranch that way. Her back was to him, and he wanted to turn her so he could see her face. But this was her story. He figured she should spin it her way.

"Okay," he said, trying not to crowd her with words.

"You already know about my marriage."

"Yeah."

"That was a mistake I swore I would never make. From the time I was a little girl, I'd always said I didn't want to get married."

"Most little girls dream of that."

She glanced over her shoulder at him. He was glad to see that she was grinning. "Who told you that?" she asked.

"I couldn't say." He shrugged. "Picked it up somewhere."

"I'm sure it's a hot topic of conversation on the rodeo circuit. Well it's true. Most little girls wait for Prince Charming to appear on his white horse and take them away to live happily ever after. I never did. Until Dave. I made the mistake of believing that could happen with him. It was a disaster."

"Yeah. So tell me why you never wanted a relationship before Dave."

"My father."

Cade heard the pain in those two words. She was starting to shake in spite of the radiating warmth of the campfire. Her teeth began to chatter.

He stood up and closed the distance between them in one stride. Without a word, he turned her toward him. Then he sat again, gently tugging her into his lap as he wrapped his arms around her. For several moments, she held herself stiff, refusing to give in to the comfort he offered.

"Let it go, P.J. Just for a little while."

Finally, she rested her head on his shoulder. "He always told me I was his best girl, his princess. Then one day, he just left. I found out later that he was having an affair with his secretary. He divorced my mother and married the other woman."

He had a feeling there was more. "What then?"

"His job transferred him out of state and eventually he stopped communicating with us."

"That's rough, but you still had your mother."

"In some ways, that's the hardest part. My mother had to go to work to support us. Sometimes she held down more than one job. My brother and I never saw her. When we did, she was too tired to be a mom. When my dad walked out, I lost both parents. What I can't forgive was the betrayal. If he'd always neglected me, I wouldn't have had expectations. But he set me up. Then he just walked. It was like I didn't exist anymore."

"It left some scars." There's a brilliant statement, McKendrick, he thought. But he was trying to encourage her to talk, to let it all out. He'd learned that from her.

She gave him a wry look, then snuggled against

him again. "What I went through is small potatoes compared to what happens to a lot of kids. I know that. And I have a good life. Which I've made for myself and my daughter. Things are just fine the way they are. I don't want to rock the boat."

"Or fall for the wrong man," he said.

"This isn't about you, Cade."

"No?" He shifted and instinctively tightened his hold on her.

"Any man is the wrong one. Look what happened the only time I let my guard down. Dave left so he would stop hurting Emily. That was noble of him, but he's still gone. And she was hurt."

"What about you?"

"Yeah. Me too. But he was my choice and I was a grown-up. Like I said before, it's a mother's job to protect her young. There are lots of things that threaten children. I won't take a chance of Emily being hurt or disappointed ever again."

"What if you're throwing away an opportunity for happiness?"

"I am happy. I don't need a man for that. Besides, I don't believe happiness is possible as a couple. It's my experience that men don't stay. When they leave, the women and children they leave behind are never the same. I will always be there for Em. I can't say the same for any man I might bring into the family dynamics." She shrugged, a small movement since he was holding her tight. "Therefore it's best if we continue to function on our own. Just the two of us."

"Even if someone comes into your life who cares about you both a lot?"

"Are you talking about love?"

Did he hear a hopeful note in her voice? Maybe.

But he heard loud and clear what she didn't say. She wanted to know how he felt about her. But he wasn't sure he knew what love was. And he would never use that word with P.J. unless he did.

"You're the English teacher. The wordmeister. I'm not sure what label to put on my feelings." When she shivered, he gently rubbed her arm. "Have you considered Emily?"

"Always."

"She wants a dad."

"She doesn't always know what's best for her. It's my job to decide that."

"Do you always know what's best?" He savored the warmth and softness of her, the sweet smell of flowers that surrounded her. She filled a place inside him that had been empty for a long time. He couldn't shake the sensation of peace when she was with him. He closed his eyes for a moment and held on tight.

"That's one of the hardest things about being a parent. Sometimes you have to take your best shot and let the chips fall where they may. Then you cross your fingers and pray."

"Is that what you did when you answered my ad?"

She nodded. "It seemed too good to be true. A job for me and summer camp for Em all rolled into one."

"So the prayers and crossed fingers worked?" He felt her tense, as if she could read his mind and knew where he was headed with this.

"So far," she said cautiously.

"It's a good place to raise children."

"Yeah. You had such a happy childhood here," she said wryly.

That stopped him. He thought back and realized it was true. He didn't remember much about his mother.

She'd died when he was younger than Emily. But his dad was always there. They hadn't had major problems until Cade's teenage years. Then they'd both taken on roles: the very strict father and the rebellious son. And he'd left home in a fit of temper. Pride kept him away. He would always regret not returning in time to know his dad as an adult. But none of that changed the fact that his childhood had been pretty good.

"Yeah," he said sincerely. "I did. This is a good place to grow up. Emily loves it here. Other than your job and the house, is there much to go back to?" She squirmed uncomfortably in his lap. "No fibs, Miss Goody Two-Shoes."

"Miss Goody Two-Shoes?" There was a smile in her voice.

"Yeah. You earned the title because I believe I took top honors for getting into trouble as a kid. So compared to me, you're pure goodness. But don't change the subject. Houses are bought and sold all the time. So what's really drawing you back to that suburb of Los Angeles?"

She frowned thoughtfully. "It's true. I don't have a lot of ties. My brother works in Phoenix. Our relationship is mostly by mail and phone now. There are people at work, but we don't see each other outside of that."

"Then what's really pulling you back?"

"Emily has friends—"

"I haven't heard her mention anyone. We both know she doesn't hold back what's on her mind. Something tells me those 'friends' aren't that important. If you gave her the choice, I'd bet a dollar to a doughnut she'd want to stay."

"This is completely impractical. I couldn't just move lock, stock and barrel on the whim of a seven-year-old."

"She's almost eight." He felt her smile.

When P.J. spoke, her tone was all-business. "I don't have a job, or a place to live."

"Schools around here need teachers. And you could—"

She pushed away from him and stood up. "Don't, Cade. Don't say it. I appreciate the spirit of your offer. Thank you. But my answer has to be no." The smile she gave him was brittle—sad—not like P.J. "We—Emily and I—only have a short time left on the ranch. Promise me you won't spoil it by bringing the subject up to me again."

He stood and looked down at her. "Okay."

She shook her head. "Say the words. No loopholes."

She really didn't trust him. The realization struck deep and painful. "I promise," he said.

"Then I'll say good-night. Emily's birthday is only a few days away and I have a lot to do to get ready." Quickly, she turned away, as if she had to escape before doing something she would regret.

"Good night." Cade watched her walk into the house. Then he sat down and looked into the fire.

He would bet his favorite saddle that P.J. wanted to take him up on his offer and stay. She'd admitted Emily was thriving. He'd never seen P.J. in a classroom, but if she looked more natural there than the kitchen or on horseback, he would eat his hat. It was safe to say she was thriving too.

Shaking his head, he wondered if he could change her mind if he told her he loved her.

Did he?

Was it love when a man couldn't think about anyone or anything but one very special woman? Was it love when he wanted to be with her all the time? Or the thought of her leaving made him ache inside? Picturing the ranch without her made a huge hole in his life. And the thought that she didn't trust him made him all the more determined to prove her wrong.

He knew she felt something for him too. But she shut her feelings down tighter than an all-girls' school when the fleet was in. At least now he knew why.

She'd been failed by one too many men. He wasn't sure he was enough to change her mind about letting a man in. But for him, she was the best thing to come along in his whole life. He wanted to find out if what he suspected was true. That she was the woman for him. He'd learned something from his dad this summer. It had taken a while for the information to get through his thick skull, but that only made the lesson more valuable.

Never give up on the ones you love.

But there wasn't much time left. How could he convince her to stay?

Chapter Eleven

"Mommy, come quick," Emily said after bursting through the kitchen door.

P.J. looked up from the birthday cake she was icing. Her child was the picture of rosy-cheeked, bright-eyed happiness. A healthy, sturdy, little girl who was vibrating with happiness. P.J. had never seen Emily as radiant as she'd been on the ranch this summer. Her heart caught as guilt rebounded through her.

How would Em react if she knew Cade had asked them to stay? P.J. was sorely tempted to accept. She'd been truthful with him that there wasn't a lot to go back for. Was it fair for her to keep the information to herself and not see how Em felt?

P.J. pushed the thought away. It was out of the question. Emily was a child. She didn't know what was best. P.J. was the adult, although leaning toward crazy to even think about staying. But the idea of leaving, of never seeing a certain cowboy again, was tearing her apart.

"What's up, sweet pea? Is it more than being eight years old today?" P.J. asked.

"It's a surprise." Emily grabbed her hand. "Come with me. Hurry."

"Can I wash my hands first?" she asked.

"You don't need clean hands, Mommy. I can't wait to show you what Mr. Cade gave me for my birthday."

As Emily pulled her out the door and up the path to the barn, P.J. felt equal parts of exhilaration and fear. She'd never seen her daughter so excited. But she had a bad feeling about what had made her that happy.

They entered the barn, going from bright sunlight to the dim interior. P.J. slowed her step as her eyes adjusted to the change. Emily continued to tug her along. "Mommy, you're not hurrying."

"Am too," she defended, gently squeezing her daughter's small hand. "Besides, you're bigger and stronger now that you turned eight. You're pulling me so hard, how can I not hurry?"

"I can't wait to show you. It's the best thing ever," the child said. "Mr. Cade says she's really mine."

What could he have given her? The smell of leather and animals confirmed that this was definitely the barn. Horses lived in a barn. *She* horses. P.J. had a bad feeling Cade hadn't given Em a year's supply of hay. And if he had, Em wouldn't be so excited about it.

"Oh, boy," P.J. whispered, desperately hoping that her suspicions were wrong.

"What did you say?"

"I said oh joy."

They stopped in front of a stall and Emily climbed

up on the slats to look at the animal inside. A beautiful chestnut horse with big, bright, intelligent brown eyes stared back.

"She's mine," Emily said beaming. "Mr. Cade gave her to me for my birthday. I named her Belle. You told me once that's French for beautiful."

"It's certainly a perfect name for her," P.J. answered.

Emily was in seventh heaven. She hadn't realized yet that this wasn't a doll she could pack up in the car and take home with them. When she did, the fall would be long and awful. Why would Cade do something like this? But of course she knew the answer. He was trying to convince her not to go back. She'd made him promise not to bring the subject up again, but he didn't swear not to get Em on his side to change her mind. The man was definitely not subtle. She couldn't decide whether to clobber him or kiss him. Why was he making this so hard for her?

If only she could throw caution to the wind and stay. She wanted to. She cared about him a lot. Everything he'd said was true. The ranch was a perfect place to raise Emily. Both of them had very few ties. Why shouldn't she stay?

The answer was the same. What if he left her?

It wasn't her physical well-being she was concerned about. She had a career. Good teachers were always in demand. But if he turned his back on her after she gave him her heart, she wasn't sure she would survive that. And he hadn't said a word about loving her.

Emily rubbed the horse's nose. "Cade said she's broken to a saddle."

P.J.'s stomach turned over. "You're not riding her

now. Not alone.'' She stopped short of saying you're only eight.

Emily shook her head and jumped down from the fence. "He said to wait. He said not to go in the stall with her until she trusts me. He said giving her treats is a good way to make friends.''

"He said a lot, didn't he?'' Fortunately Emily didn't pick up on her sarcasm. She was walking away. "Where are you going?'' P.J. said to her daughter's back.

Em glanced over her shoulder, a mildly annoyed look on her face. "To get her a treat. Belle and I are going to be good friends.''

Leaving the ranch and her new best friend was going to break the child's heart. When she got hold of Cade, she planned to give him an earful.

"Em?''

"What, Mommy?'' This time something in her tone must have registered because the child stopped and turned to face her.

P.J. crossed the short distance to her daughter and went down on one knee in the straw. She stared into green eyes that were excited and now just a bit wary. "Em, I don't know if you should be here with the horse alone.''

"You're here, Mom.''

"I have something to do.''

"But it's my birthday. She's my horse. I want to stay with her.''

"I know.'' She sighed.

This was just a small preview of what it would be like when Emily had to face the fact that she couldn't keep her best birthday present. She had to hand it to Cade. The Princess of Pout would be a powerful ally in his campaign to get her to stick around. But it wouldn't work.

"Sweetie, I can't leave you alone, and I can't stay. There's something I have to do right away." The sooner, the better she added under her breath.

She needed to keep Em from getting too attached to the animal. Then she noticed the adoring look her little girl sent to the horse. It was probably already too late. But before she broke Emily's heart, she wanted to talk to Cade and find out what he'd actually said to the child.

Steve walked in from the other side of the barn that connected to the corral. "I'll stay with her, P.J.," he said. He'd obviously overheard their difference of opinion.

"If Steve's here can I stay with Belle? Is it okay, Mom?"

No it wasn't okay. Nothing was okay. Her life would never be okay again. Thanks to Cade. How could she tell Emily to hold back? To not put her heart on the line? To not be disappointed and disillusioned? Those were hard lessons. P.J. would never forget the pain. She was doing her best to keep Em from feeling the worst sort of hurt, the kind that followed the shattering of childish dreams.

"Sweetie, I know you're anxious to make friends with the horse—"

"Her name is Belle." Emily's bottom lip stuck out slightly. Her alter ego was on the rise.

Darn it. Why hadn't he said something before doing this? She would never forgive him if he spoiled Em's birthday.

"I have to talk to Cade before you get too friendly

with her. Are you sure you didn't misunderstand that she's yours?''

Emily gave her a disgusted look. "I'm not a little kid any more. I'm eight, Mom."

"I know, sweetie."

It would be too awful if the gift she received for turning eight was cynicism. Still, P.J. couldn't bring herself to break the bad news yet. Maybe Emily had misunderstood. Maybe he'd just said she could ride the animal on her birthday. Maybe he hadn't given it to her for her very own.

This was the same man who had been so obviously angry when she related the story of Em's no-show father on her fifth birthday. Cade had said she'd known enough heartbreak. Would he set her up for more in an effort to get what he wanted? The thought made her angry. On the other hand, she wanted very much to believe he hadn't done anything underhanded. She tried not to assume the worst, she needed to get it straight from the horse's mouth, so to speak.

She looked up at Steve. "Do you know where Cade is?"

He nodded. "He's checking the fences up behind the house."

P.J. smiled at him then met Emily's gaze. "You stay here with Steve and mind what he says. He'll look after you."

"Okay, Mom."

Cade brushed the sweat from his forehead, then rested his arm on the fence post. He saw P.J. in the distance, walking quickly toward him. From this far away, he couldn't see her expression, but something told him she wasn't happy.

"I wonder what put the hitch in her git-along?" he said to himself.

As he waited, he admired her stride, and the way she filled out a pair of jeans. Over the summer he'd gone from tolerating her presence to anticipating the sight of her every day. There would be a big hole in his life when she was gone. How was he going to get used to the emptiness? Would he ever get used to it, or would he always miss her? He suspected the latter was true.

She stopped beside him and took a deep breath. "How could you do this?" she asked furiously.

"Do what?" How could he have upset her? He hadn't seen her much in the last couple days. She'd avoided him like bad news ever since that night by the campfire.

"Don't play dumb. It doesn't suit you. I'm talking about the horse." She crossed her arms over her chest. "Before I say anything I might have to retract later, let me make sure I understand the situation. Did you in fact give my daughter a horse for her birthday?"

"Yeah."

"No misunderstanding. You didn't just tell her she could ride the animal for the day, then give her back?"

"She understood me right. After all, she's eight," he said grinning. He figured when Emily was a full grown woman she might fudge on her age, but right now the whole world knew how old she was. "That is her very own horse. I wanted to wait until—"

"And just where is my daughter supposed to keep her very own horse?"

"In the barn, or maybe the corral."

She shook her head. "Oddly enough, our house doesn't have a barn or a corral."

He rubbed his chin. "You don't say."

"Don't you dare turn into the strong, silent type. I want some answers. I know what you're trying to do."

"Then you have all the answers." Apparently everyone but him was innocent until proven guilty. She'd already made up her mind he'd done a hanging offense.

"I just want you to confirm my suspicions."

"It's proper to give someone a gift on their birthday. Right?"

"Yes, but—"

"This is Emily's birthday, right?"

"Of course it is. That doesn't—"

"That horse is definitely a filly. But she's no shallow standard of feminine beauty. Something you don't want Em to have. Am I wrong?"

"The horse is not an overly commercialized doll, that's for sure. And therein lies the problem."

"Enlighten me."

"As if you need enlightening. That's a horse, for Pete's sake! We can't take her home. And it will break Em's heart to leave her behind. She's already named the animal, Cade."

"I'm flattered. She told me she named the horse Belle."

"This is not the time to flex your sense of humor. I'm not in the mood. And I repeat, how could you do this?"

He stared at her. "I thought Emily would like her."

"Don't toy with me," she said, pointing at him.

"It's the truth." He stared into P.J.'s eyes and recognized the hurt. It was the only thing keeping his temper in check. "I just wanted to make her birthday memorable. That's all."

"Then you've succeeded. This is one I'll never forget. Or Em either when the trauma sets in. Did you think about where the horse will live? Or how much it costs to feed her?"

"I'll board her here."

"Did it occur to you that Emily would not be okay with riding off into the sunset—in a compact car."

He pushed his hat off his forehead. "Spit it out, P.J. What's really bugging you? Are you accusing me of manipulating the situation?"

"I couldn't have put it better myself."

"And what could I possibly get from giving Emily a horse?"

"An ally to convince me to stay here."

He went completely still as her words sank in. The idea hadn't crossed his mind, at least not consciously. But he wasn't sure that her allegation didn't have a grain of truth to it.

"Aren't you going to deny it?"

"Would you believe me if I did?" he asked, hedging.

"I don't want to jump to any conclusions."

"You already have. Your mind is made up. Judge, jury and executioner. You're convinced that I would use that little girl to persuade you not to go."

"Didn't you?"

"Emily is a natural with horses. She wanted one. I have one." He was still dancing around her accusation. "And I was trying to make up for her not getting a pony ride on her fifth birthday. In a small way," he added.

"A small way?" She caught her top lip between her teeth, and he watched her fighting both anger and tears. "There's nothing small about a horse."

"As horses go, she is small. That's why I picked her for Em."

"But it will break her heart when she realizes we can't take Belle home with us."

"You only live a couple hours away by car. She's welcome to visit any time she wants."

"So it never entered your mind that she'll want to do that all the time? Or that she would work on me to bring her back? Or try to convince me not to go?"

There was enough truth in what she said to make him uncomfortable. He hadn't done it intentionally, but the result was the same. He had used Emily. His father had always counted on the worst from him. And he never disappointed. It was nice to know some things never changed, he thought grimly. He had risen to P.J.'s low expectations about men and relationships, and proven her right to avoid him like the plague.

He would never have deliberately hurt her, or Emily. "I'm sorry, P.J. Guess I didn't think it all the way through."

"You sure didn't, cowboy. Now I have to face my daughter and be the bad guy."

He shook his head. "No, you don't. That's my job."

He might believe it was his job to be the resident black hat, P.J. thought, but it hadn't escaped her notice that he wouldn't be the hatchet man on Em's birthday. He waited until the following day to tell her the bad news.

After dinner, he took her out onto the front porch and sat on the swing. P.J. stood by the railing, on call for moral support, if the need arose. For either or both of them. Light filtering through the window high-lighted Emily's face, worship in her eyes as she looked up at her hero. Only Cade's profile was visible from P.J.'s vantage point, but it was enough to make her heart pound. The more he tried to convince her he was pond scum, the more she wanted to wrap her arms around him and stay with him forever.

He cleared his throat, the only outward sign that he was at all nervous. "Emily, we need to talk about Belle."

"Okay. I bet you want to tell me how to take care of her."

"Sort of. It's about what's best for her. You want her to be happy, don't you?"

"Oh, yes." She clapped her hands together, then dropped them in her lap. "I love her."

"Do you have a place to keep her at home?"

The little girl thought for a moment, and a frown deepened. "It's a condo-minimum and there's lots of sidewalks."

He smiled at her misuse of the word. "That's good."

"Yeah. But we don't have a very big backyard. Mom said I couldn't get a dog because there wasn't room to run. And it wouldn't be fair to an animal."

He nodded his understanding. "You know Belle has a special diet. She can't have table scraps or peo-ple food or anything you can get at the grocery store."

"She needs ranch stuff."

He nodded seriously. "That's right. Is there one close by? Maybe where Belle could live?"

Emily's forehead wrinkled as she gave that some thought. Finally, she shook her head. "I don't think so. We live in the city."

He nodded. "And even if there was, it might cost a lot to keep her there."

Emily glanced at P.J. "Mom works awful hard. She's always doing extra jobs and stuff. She's pretty tired. I guess it's not easy to feed us."

The words tore at P.J.'s heart. The way the muscle in Cade's cheek contracted, she knew he was having a difficult time with this too. Then Emily crawled into his lap. He went still for several moments before his arms slowly went around the little girl.

"Your mom loves you and she wants you to be happy, the same thing you want for Belle." He stopped for a moment, and the muscle in his cheek contracted. "Even if there was a place big enough to keep her, she wouldn't have any friends and it might make her sad."

Awed, P.J. stared at Cade. For a man who said he wasn't very good with kids, he was doing a masterful job. He was leading Emily straight where he wanted her. Guiding her to the conclusion that the horse would be better off here. And he'd already gotten her to say that she wanted Belle to be happy. P.J. hadn't thought it was possible, but he might actually pull this off without upsetting her too much.

Emily brushed the hair off her forehead, then rested her cheek against his chest. "I wouldn't mind leaving my friends if I could live on a ranch."

If P.J. didn't know better, she would think he'd put her up to that.

He shot P.J. a quick glance, saying with a look that he'd read her thoughts and was not guilty. Then he continued. "So you understand that leaving would be hard for her. Going from a ranch where she's happy, to a place she would be miserable."

Not to mention breaking every zoning law ever written, P.J. thought. But a child wouldn't understand that.

Emily sighed. "I don't want her to be sad. I guess I better give her back to you." There was a tremor in her voice.

"No. She's yours."

"If I leave her here, could I come back and ride her?"

Cade saw her lips quiver and felt lower than a snake's belly. "Any time you want. It's only a couple hours' drive. Maybe your mom can bring you sometime."

Emily shot her a hopeful look. "Can I, Mommy?"

"We'll see," she answered, looking ready to cry.

Cade felt like a world-class jerk. He'd thought the gift was a good thing, but he'd managed to hurt them both. It wasn't supposed to be like this. It was supposed to be just a summer job. When your work shift was over, most times you were happy to go home. How had everything turned out so upside down?

Fighting tears, she forced a smile as she added, "A visit is a possibility."

"Good," he said in that deep, seductive voice that raised gooseflesh on her arms. "I'm going to need a cook next June."

Was he saying what she thought? "Are you going to do another summer camp?" she asked.

"Yeah." He met Emily's gaze. "I'm going to need someone to help out again. What do you think?"

"I think you need Mommy and me to teach you about boys." She put her small arms around him as far as they would go and hugged for all she was worth. He returned the gesture with a show of tenderness that brought a lump to P.J.'s throat.

"So what do you want to do with Belle, Em?" he asked in a voice she'd never heard from him before. The deep tone was thick with emotion.

"I want to leave her here with you. She'll miss me. And I'll miss her a lot too. But she'll be happy with you. I know you'll take good care of her."

"I will. Promise."

"Thanks, Mr. Cade." She arched up and kissed his cheek. "She's the best birthday present I ever got." Emily looked at her. "Mom, can I go inside now and play Scrabble? We only have five more nights here. I'm going to miss Todd, and Mark. But mostly Steve. I want to spend as much time with them as I can. Before we go home."

"Permission granted, sweet pea," P.J. said.

When the little girl had gone into the house, Cade studied her for several moments. "What are you thinking?" he asked.

"That you speak with forked tongue."

"Huh?"

"You told me you're not very good father material. A bald-faced falsehood, cowboy. What I just saw was sheer genius at work."

Puzzled, he scratched his head. "So you're not mad at me anymore?"

"You managed to give her a horse and take it away and she still adores you."

"Nah."

"Don't be so modest. It was nothing short of brilliant. And she's still crazy about you."

And so am I.

As hard as she fought against it, the proof stood right in front of her—six feet two inches of rugged cowboy. His intense look made her heart pound. She prayed for him to take her in his arms and change her mind about leaving.

"I guess I'll see if I can get in on this game too," he said instead. "You want to join us?"

"No, thanks. Good night, Cade."

"'Night."

He left her alone with her thoughts. Apparently it was only wishful thinking that he'd had ulterior motives in giving Em a horse. It was bad enough that she'd jumped to the wrong conclusion, but she realized he was sticking to his word. He hadn't said another thing to try to convince her to stay.

He was exactly what she thought, an honorable man. This was a heck of a time for her to see the truth.

She was head over heels in love with Cade McKendrick.

Chapter Twelve

"You're packing." Cade lounged in her bedroom doorway, watching her. The time between Em's birthday and D-day, departure day, had passed far too quickly.

"Yes," she said, putting the last of Emily's clothes into the suitcase. Was there regret in his voice? Or was it just wishful thinking on her part? "The boys are going back in the morning, so you don't need me anymore."

Tell me I'm wrong. Change my mind, she thought. If he touched her. If he took her in his arms and told her he loved her, she wouldn't be able to leave. If he still wanted her to stay, that could make the difference.

"I talked to Steve," he said. "I told him he's welcome to live here with me on the ranch. I offered to run interference with the social worker."

"Oh, Cade—" Tears welling in her eyes stopped her. Blubbering was so unattractive and she was sink-ing toward it. But how could she not? He'd come a long way from the man who didn't want any part of this program or the kids. "Your father would be so proud of you."

"I hope so." He shrugged and folded his arms over his chest.

"What did Steve say?"

"He wants to live with his mom, try to make it work with her." For a moment, regret darkened Cade's blue eyes. "I told him if things get rough to call. He's a good kid."

"You're a good man."

I love you. But the words stayed in her head and her heart.

"I want to—"

"Tomorrow morning—"

They both started to talk at once.

"Ladies first," he said.

"Always the gentleman cowboy." She stared at his face, memorizing the rugged bone structure, the lines beside his nose and mouth that deepened when he was tired, the intensity in his eyes. When she grew lonely, she would pull out the mental picture and hoped it would be enough.

She cleared her throat, swallowing the emotion. "I just wanted to say thanks for everything."

"This is goodbye?" he asked, sounding a little surprised.

She nodded. "You're driving the boys back to the social worker tomorrow. I'm going home. In case we miss each other, I wanted to tell you how much I appreciate your kindness to Emily and me."

This was the coward's way out. With a house full of kids, she wasn't likely to say or do anything stupid.

And she needed the farewells over with before she couldn't say them at all.

Cade wanted to shake her, or kiss her. Or both. He couldn't say so long, ma'am. Been nice knowing you. He refused to accept that it was over between them. Somehow he had to convince P.J. that she and Emily belonged here with him. But how? He needed time to think. With an uphill battle like P. J. Kirkland, he had to find just the right words to persuade her that he was different, that he wouldn't let her down, that he would never leave her. The long drive back from town after he dropped the boys off would give him the chance to prepare his speech.

"We'll do this tomorrow," he said quickly.

"There won't be an opportunity. I just wanted you to know—"

"We'll make the opportunity." He looked at her.

There were questions in her big, brown eyes. There was emotion too. He hoped it was all about him. This was the most important thing he'd ever done and he didn't want to blow it. He'd finally ditched the screw-up kid he'd been. P.J. had finally convinced him he was a good man. Now, more than ever, he had to be. He'd waited a lifetime for P.J. He needed to do this right, when it was just him and her—the two of them alone. She had to know his feelings went deep. This was about the woman she was—the woman he loved.

But he couldn't just blurt it out that way. She was skittish enough. He didn't want to scare her off.

"Wait for me tomorrow, P.J."

"I'm leaving at ten," she said again.

"I won't hold you up." Unless you want to be, he added silently. "Promise me you won't go until we have a chance to talk."

"You mean say goodbye."

"Whatever. Just promise me. Don't go until I get back from taking the guys. I should be back by ten."

"Okay."

P.J. paid the clerk at the convenience store/service station closest to the ranch. She'd pulled in to fill her gas tank for the long ride home. After paying, she walked outside and stopped beside her car, peeking inside. Em was still asleep, worn out from crying because she hadn't been able to say goodbye to Cade. He hadn't arrived back at the appointed time.

He hadn't even called. If he'd only phoned, she could believe that he cared. Obviously he didn't. So what else was new, she thought trying to ignore the sound of her heart breaking. She realized she should have expected it, but she'd hoped Cade was different.

P.J. hadn't been able to bear waiting any longer. But Emily threw a fit that did the Princess of Pout proud. She was too little to understand that P.J. was trying to spare her from being hurt in the long run. If only there was a way to do that for herself. If she lived for a hundred years, she had a bad feeling that the pain of leaving Cade would still be intolerable.

This was the right thing, she told herself for the umpteenth time. This was best for Em, and for her. But if it was right, then why did it feel as if she'd received a failing grade on something she'd put her heart and soul into?

"If I meant anything to him—" She caught her lip between her teeth, trying to hold back the tears. "If *we* meant anything to him," she whispered, "he would have been there to say goodbye. Like he promised."

Just then she heard the squeal of tires and looked past her car to see a truck tearing into the parking lot. The vehicle looked a lot like Cade's. When the driver got out, slammed the door—hard—and came around, she saw that it *was* him. Her heart started to pound.

He stomped over to her and she noticed dirt all over his face and clothes. He pointed at her and said, "I have something to say to you."

"You came," she said.

He went on as if he hadn't heard. "You preach second chances for everyone else, but I don't rate even a first one."

"What are you talking about?" She couldn't resist touching his face, brushing at the smudge there. It wouldn't rub off. "What is this?"

"Grease."

"What happened?" she asked.

"Flat tire."

"Are the boys all right?"

"It happened after I dropped them off with the social worker. That took longer than I thought. She wanted to talk about next summer. I was on my way back when the tire blew."

"Why didn't you call?"

"I did. There was no answer."

The expression on his face was so bleak, she felt his pain. "I paced out front a lot. Guess I didn't hear the phone ring."

"You were so sure I would let you down, you couldn't even wait?"

"I waited two hours."

"I'm only ten minutes behind you. What we have isn't worth waiting two hours and ten lousy minutes?"

"You were actually going to come back?" It was half question, half statement, but all-surprise.

"It's my ranch."

"I know that. I was referring to an emotional rendezvous. You actually planned to come back?"

He nodded. "I actually *did* come back. But you were gone. You didn't trust me."

"You mean you were really going to do what you said? You were going to keep your promise to say goodbye?"

"I was coming back, but not to say that."

"What then?"

"I didn't say it last night because I needed time to figure out the right words to ask you to marry me."

She put a trembling hand to her mouth. "Oh, Cade—"

"Damn it. I love you."

The sun was warm, but she went cold all over. He *loved* her? She was afraid to believe that. She just couldn't bring herself to expect the best. She prepared for the worst and that's what she got.

"Oh, Cade. I'm sorry. I was just afraid. It hurts too much to count on someone."

"It only hurts if they let you down. I would never do that. To you or Em."

She stopped, swallowing the lump in her throat. This wasn't a memorized speech. He was speaking from his heart. "You've always done what you said. You've never broken a promise. You've never given me a reason to think that you would."

"Then why didn't you cut me some slack? You couldn't wait ten lousy minutes?"

"There's no reason on God's green earth you

should believe me, but I hope and pray that you'll listen.''

"Shoot," he said, still wearing that dark intense look.

"Leaving you was the hardest thing I've ever done. The truth is it wasn't you I don't trust. It's myself.''

"Now you've lost me," he said shaking his head. "Spit it out, P.J. Straight and easy. I didn't sleep much last night, so I'm a little slow. What are you telling me?''

"I'm stubborn.''

"There's a news flash.''

"Once I get an idea into my head, it's hard for me to let go.''

"Then I darn well hope your point is that you've got me in your head.''

She nodded. "But old habits die hard. I reverted to type and pushed you away. My head wasn't the problem.''

"What is?''

"My heart. I've been afraid to trust it to anyone. I don't know how to love.''

He laughed, a short, sharp sound without humor. "You? Miss Goody Two-Shoes? The woman who protects kids' rights like a mother lion?''

She shrugged. "Kids are easy. It's this man/woman thing that baffles me. I don't know how to do that. I don't like trying things I don't know how to do.''

"Remember how glad you were that I made you try horseback riding?''

She nodded. "But I could survive if Hunny turned her back and walked away from me.'' Her voice cracked and she waited a moment before continuing. "I left because I was afraid to see you one more time.

I knew if I did, no way could I turn my back and ride off into the sunset. And I wouldn't make it if you let me down.''

He grinned for the first time since he'd arrived with a squeal of tires and spraying gravel. The dark look vanished.

Cade gripped her upper arms. "Are you telling me—"

"I'm a coward."

"What else?"

"The slime of the earth," she said.

"And?"

"If you were smart, you would wash your hands of me."

He looked at the black marks he'd left on her sleeves, then stared ruefully at his hands. "The only thing I'm washing my hands of is this grease." Then he stared into her eyes and the intense expression returned. "I want to hold you in my arms and never let you go. Say it, P.J. Tell me what I need to hear."

She looked up at him, meeting his gaze. Needing to see his expression. "I hope you can forgive me."

"For what?"

"I didn't give you a second chance. But I'm hoping you're a nicer person than I am and you'll do as I say, not as I do."

"Second chance?" he asked.

"Yeah. I hope you can—"

He cupped her face in his hands and stared into her eyes. His determination to convince her of his sincerity came through loud and clear. "You're not on probation, P.J. This isn't an experiment. I love you with everything I've got in me."

The tears she'd been holding back spilled over. "Oh, Cade—"

"Thanks to you, I've got the ranch now. The hell of it is, when I got there and you and Em were gone, it hit me between the eyes. The ranch, the land, the animals, the whole ball of wax wouldn't mean a damn thing if you weren't there to share it with. I love you, P.J. There's nothing to forgive."

"Yes, there is."

"Okay. Have it your way." He held up his hand. "I swear on my father's love that I will never turn my back on you. I will be there for you as long as you want me which I hope will be as long as I live. I will do my best to never disappoint you. And I will love Em like my own. I'll forgive you if you can look me in the eye and tell me you believe that."

She nodded, her throat too full of emotion to form words.

"Say it," he said.

"I believe you. I trust you. I love you. Because that speech wasn't rehearsed. You didn't need time to find the right thing to say. You came after me. You spoke from your heart. That's all I ever want or need."

The relief, wonder, and joy on his face when she said the words convinced her as nothing else could.

"Okay." His voice cracked, a sign of his deep emotion.

He lowered his head and touched his lips to hers. Every kiss she'd shared with Cade was filled with passion. This one was no less so, but there was something else. Promise. The pledge of a lifetime of support, laughter and love. The assurance she needed that he would always be there for her.

"Does this mean we get to stay?" Emily's sleepy voice came from the car.

He grinned at P.J. "I need to ask someone's permission to marry you."

P.J. smiled back. "You could wind up with your backside in the dirt, cowboy. She's tough as leather and sharp as nails."

Cade loosened his hold on P.J. but grabbed her hand as he moved to the open car window. "Emily," his voice cracked again, endearing him to her even more. "Would it be all right with you if I married your mom?"

The little girl frowned thoughtfully for a moment. "Does it mean we get to stay on the ranch?"

"Yeah."

"And you'd still be a cowboy?"

"Yeah."

"And would you be my daddy?"

"If you want me to."

She smiled and clapped her hands together. "Yaaay. I finally got what I wanted for my birthday. A cowboy for my dad."

He opened the car door and lifted her out. She gave him a hug. He pulled P.J. into his embrace and said, "And I've got what I always wanted."

"A family?" P.J. asked, confirming what she'd known all along.

He nodded. "When you answered my ad, I never dreamed that things would turn out like this," he said, meeting her look with a very satisfied one of his own.

"You wanted a cook."

"Little did I know her specialty would be love."

"And I plan to dish it out for as long as you live, cowboy."

"Amen to that," he said, lowering his mouth to hers for confirmation that was more eloquent without words.

* * * * *

Don't miss talented author Teresa Southwick's
next sweet love story,
AND THEN HE KISSED ME,
coming to
Silhouette Romance, November 1999.

Silhouette ROMANCE™

twins
on the doorstep

STELLA BAGWELL

continues her wonderful stories of the Murdocks
in Romance & *Special Edition!*

MILLIONAIRE ON HER DOORSTEP—May 1999
(SR#1368)

Then be sure to follow this miniseries when it
leaps into Silhouette Special Edition® with
Sheriff Ethan Hamilton, the son of Rose and
Harlan. Discover what happens when a small
New Mexico town finds out that...

PENNY PARKER'S PREGNANT!—July 1999
(SE#1258)

Judge Penny Parker longed to be a mother, but
the lonely judge needed more than the sheriff's
offer of a "trial" marriage....

Look for a new Murdocks short story in
Silhouette's Mother's Day collection, coming out in
May 2000

Available at your favorite retail outlet.

Silhouette®

If you enjoyed what you just read,
then we've got an offer you can't resist!

Take 2 bestselling
love stories FREE!
Plus get a FREE surprise gift!

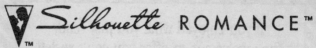

Available July 1999 from Silhouette Books...

AGENT OF
THE BLACK WATCH
by BJ JAMES

The World's Most Eligible Bachelor:
Secret-agent lover Kieran O'Hara was on a desperate mission.
His objective: Anything but marriage!

Kieran's mission pitted him against a crafty killer...and
the prime suspect's beautiful sister. For the first time in his
career, Kieran's instincts as a man overwhelmed his lawman's
control...and he claimed Beau Anna Cahill as his lover. But
would this innocent remain in his bed once she learned his
secret agenda?

Each month, Silhouette Books brings you an
irresistible bachelor in these all-new, original
stories. Find out how the sexiest, most-sought-after men
are finally caught....
Available at your favorite retail outlet.

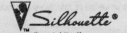

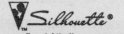

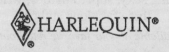